COVER GIRL & OTHER STORIES OF FLY-FISHERMEN IN MAINE

COVER GIRL & OTHER STORIES OF FLY-FISHERMEN IN MAINE

J.H. Hall

iUniverse, Inc.
New York Lincoln Shanghai

Cover Girl & Other Stories of Fly-Fishermen in Maine

Copyright © 2005 by J.H. Hall

All rights reserved. No part of this book may be used or reproduced by any means, graphic, electronic, or mechanical, including photocopying, recording, taping or by any information storage retrieval system without the written permission of the publisher except in the case of brief quotations embodied in critical articles and reviews.

iUniverse books may be ordered through booksellers or by contacting:

iUniverse
2021 Pine Lake Road, Suite 100
Lincoln, NE 68512
www.iuniverse.com
1-800-Authors (1-800-288-4677)

"The River Dwight" was first published in *TriQuarterly*, a publication of Northwestern University. "Michaud's Fine Rods & Flies" was first published in *FlyRod & Reel*. A slightly different version of "Thomaston U." was first published in *Carolina Quarterly*.

ISBN-13: 978-0-595-37288-1 (pbk)
ISBN-13: 978-0-595-81685-9 (ebk)
ISBN-10: 0-595-37288-0 (pbk)
ISBN-10: 0-595-81685-1 (ebk)

Printed in the United States of America

For Preston & Evan

and for Patricia Dickson

With special thanks to Stuart S. Smith, Master Maine Guide
& master raconteur

Contents

Cover Girl 1
The River Dwight 99
Whitcomb's Raid 118
Michaud's Fine Rods & Flies 129
Thomaston U. 144

Cover Girl

1

Conrad Larue and Brash Whitcomb were drinking beer in the Black Toad and trying to calculate how much longer they could afford to fish before they had to break down and take some paying customers. Spring fishing around Greenville was simply too good to waste on flatlanders.

Whitcomb and Larue ran a guide service, but like most Maine Guides worthy of the name, they much preferred fishing to guiding. It used to be that they could earn enough in July and August to support their admittedly modest life style for the rest of the year, but according to Murl, their friend and business manager, bookings were way down for their "money months." Murl had an apartment in town with a telephone and computer, and he had a knack for finances. He had identified two major factors accounting for the decline of business: The Movie and Spike Jackson.

The Movie, *A River Runs Through It,* attracted hordes of newcomers to fly-fishing, but also increased clients' expectations—bad news for guides like Whitcomb and Larue. Lowered expectations, or, as they called them, "altered expectations," were an integral part of their fishing package. But since The Movie, catching a few small trout in a lovely setting wasn't enough. These newly minted fly-fishers wanted poetry in motion—back-lit shots of graceful casts, large trout taking to the air in graceful leaps. And for guides, they expected Brad Pitt—clean-cut, handsome, and roguish. Whitcomb was roguish enough by any measure, but his fist-bent nose detracted from his looks. And Larue, while potentially decent looking in an angular, anorectic way, adamantly refused to trim his shaggy hair or beard in order to satisfy some city slicker's phony idea of how a fly-fishing guide ought to look. Larue and Whitcomb were not without principles. But, sadly, neither were their clients, and their clients' current expectations included a "gourmet" lunch.

"What the devil is 'gourmet' lunch?" Whitcomb inquired the first time he heard the term.

"Beats the hell out of me," Larue said.

The "shore lunch" had a rich tradition in Maine, and in the old days invariably meant freshly caught fish fried over an open fire against a backdrop of spruce and fir beneath a deep blue sky. But over the years a scarcity of trout and a changing ethic made eating fish anathema to most fly-fishermen. Which suited Larue and Whitcomb just fine; they supported Catch & Release and didn't much like cooking. So in their hands the "shore lunch" had come to mean a roast beef Italian, or turkey or ham Italian (whatever was available at the Trading Post), a large bag of chips, barbecue *and* plain (because they aimed, within reason, to please), topped off with an assortment of candy bars and cookies for dessert. For beverage they offered a selection of soda, fruit drinks, and tap water. For years nobody complained. Then Brash and Conrad started getting looks, even comments, such as "When was this sandwich actually made?"

"Whatever it says on the wrapper," was their stock reply, their point, implied with tone of voice and a look, being, "This is not a restaurant, dude, and we aren't chefs." Then along came Spike Jackson and his "gourmet" shore lunches to ruin it all.

Their friend Murl did some market research and determined that the essential ingredients, the sine qua non, of the "gourmet" shore lunch were wine and bottled water instead of soda, sprouts instead of lettuce, and fruit and cheese instead of candy bars. "Big freaking deal," Brash said. "We can do that."

So they went Spike Jackson one better and changed their business card, which Murl created and regularly updated on his computer, to read "Super Gourmet Shore Lunches," whatever that meant. Murl said what it meant was more business, a healthier bottom line.

Unfortunately it didn't mean that *much* more business, and one winter Brash had to break down and cut and sell firewood to make ends meet, and Conrad made maple syrup, but neither felt right about it. They were *Master Guides,* and that sort of work was beneath them. For Brash and Conrad collecting unemployment was more honorable than performing what they called "ordinary work." Great artists of the Renaissance had patrons. Why shouldn't they?

Brash, though not a traditionally religious man, said that they were approaching the "end of times." The whole business of flyfishing had become so rarified, so effete, that it was just about over. TAG—touch and go—fishing was but the most recent sign of the apocalypse. As he explained it, the essence of Catch & Release was *catching.* "You can't release what you don't catch." And releasing trout was how this new breed got "their rocks off," as he put it. It made them feel good, and Brash was all for feeling good, however it might be achieved (and he had the twelve step achievement badges to prove it).

The first threat to Catch & Release was barbless hooks. Some smart aleck determined that removing the hook's barb made the releasing much easier. The part he overlooked was, it made the *catching* harder. And it just got worse. The next ethical advance was to break off the entire hook. The first time Brash heard it, he thought it was a joke. But no, these people were serious. The idea was that since the "take" was the most exciting part of the fishing experience—absolutely true—then the other, the setting of the hook, the playing and landing of the fish, the measuring, and the photo—all, of course, terribly traumatic for the trout—could be dispensed with entirely.

"The end is near," Brash said into his beer. "I can feel it coming. One day, it will be enough to just sit beside the river and think pretty thoughts about nature. Who needs a freaking guide for that? Even Spike Jackson could be out of business, though knowing him, he'd probably sell 'gourmet' pretty thoughts, thoughts prettier than you could think up on your own."

Larue pondered bubbles at the bottom of his glass. "I don't see it that way," he said.

"Naw? Well, you've always been a Pollyanna, haven't you? With you the glass is always half full."

"Not this one." He lifted his glass and looked around for the waitress. "Anyway, I think you're overlooking an important factor. Money! Think about it. You got makers of the rods, reels, lines, flies, clothing, gear—hooks! You got Orvis, and Bean's, and Cabelas, Sage, Simms, Mustad—they all got a stake in this."

Brash tipped his head side to side, weighing his friend's argument. "You might have a point," he said. "God, I hope you're right. The day they turn fly-fishing into golf or tennis or—god forbid—white water rafting, that's the day I get out."

"Amen," said Conrad. Fly-fishing was a blood sport, even under the best of circumstances. Even in The Movie, people kept and ate their catch, though, of course, they didn't show it on film or nowadays it would've gotten an X-rating. Even when you released the fish, a few died. Fishing was life or death, like bull fighting. And if you wanted to argue that it was only life or death for the fish, then obviously you hadn't paid attention to the obituary columns: every spring half a dozen Maine fishermen, ignoring the hazards of frigid water, died in the pursuit of their quarry. Nowadays fishing was more dangerous than hunting.

Having arrived at a sort of truce with the apocalypse, Whitcomb and Larue ordered more beer. The young waitress gave them a skeptical look. "Quite a tab you boys are running up this evening," she said.

When she was out of earshot, Brash said, "That *never* used to happen."

"I never thought I'd see the day when someone would have the audacity to question *our* credit."

Then, to add injury to insult, Spike Jackson strode into the Black Toad, as if he owned the place. He was a wiry six-footer, blonde, and handsome—two more strikes against him—wearing a cowboy hat and hip waders. The two guides leaned so far over their little table that the tops of their heads almost collided. "What a jerk," Brash muttered into his beer.

As they saw it, Spike Jackson was bringing the big business mentality to Maine fly-fishing: the hard sell, the drift-boat, the big money, the fifty–fish days, not to mention the "gourmet" shore lunch. Jackson even cultivated the cowboy look. That might have worked on the Henry's Fork, but not in Greenville, Maine. True, Greenville retained a frontier feel and charm, but it was the *Eastern* frontier; it was log drives, float planes, and fly-in fishing. The Black Toad's knotty-pine walls were decorated with pikes, peaveys, pulp hooks, and huge two-man saws. The table tops were cross sections of old-growth pine, lacquered to a hard sheen. The log drives had turned the river beds into picket fences of pulp, and the river bends into dense thickets of tree-length timber. The drives were ended in the 1970s. Now the logs were trucked to the mills. Trucks meant new roads and access to previously remote waters. Then came the kiss of death: the Delorme Atlas, with microscopic details of logging roads, gates, and trails. Now everybody with four-wheel drive was his own guide. Then Spike Jackson arrived on the scene. The man might have been deaf and blind to the subtleties of Maine culture, but he definitely had a head for business. He redefined the fly-fishing product.

Brash and Conrad were of the "secret knowledge" school of guides, the "old school," outmoded by new roads and better maps. Spike had a business degree. He knew how to push product, how to market the Maine woods, and most of all, how to market himself as celebrity guide, a guide you wanted to be able to say you had fished with. And he created needs—for better service, etc.—that only *he* was qualified to satisfy. As a result, he had plenty of business, but the others didn't. He also had the perfect Chamber of Commerce personality. Most people found it hard not to like him, though Brash and Conrad did not find it particularly difficult. "Doesn't even tie his own flies!" Brash said, as if this were a major character flaw.

Spike worked his way through the long narrow bar, like a campaigning politician, shaking hands, saying "hi" to people, half of whom he didn't even know, but making the other half think, "Boy that Spike Jackson knows everybody. You must have to book him *months* ahead."

When Spike finally squeezed past their table, Brash didn't even deign to look up, but Conrad flashed a big insincere smile and said, "How's fishing big guy?"

"Great!" he said. "Fishing is excellent."

"Yeah, right," Brash muttered, *still* not looking up, as a matter of principle.

"No, really, we hammered 'em on the Outlet," he said, loud enough for several tables of potential customers to hear. "How're you boys doing?"

Larue made a non-committal gesture with his hand. In fact, they were doing all right—this time of year it was hard not to—but they damn well weren't going to talk about it in public.

"A little caddis nymph," Spike said, holding his fingers just far enough to fit a size #18 fly between them. "Behind a big black stonefly. Whooee!"

Brash finally just couldn't tolerate this conduct any longer said, "Well, why don't you just announce it to the whole eff-ing world? You want us to get you a loud speaker?"

"What?"

"Your trouble is, you don't know the difference between a prostitute and a slut. Prostitution is an honorable profession. But to give it away," Brash said shaking his head, "that's just cheap, man"

"A rising tide raises all ships," Spike said.

"What the fuck is that supposed to mean?"

"Why don't you ask your buddy Murl to explain it. I'm sure he understands."

"Screw you!" Brash said, rising from his chair.

"Hey, hey, hey," Conrad said, standing to intercept his friend. "Don't mind him," he said to Spike. "Tough day. We lost some good ones."

"Customers or fish?" Spike said.

"Ha, that's a good one," Conrad said. "You have yourself a nice evening."

Spike stood there long enough for them to understand that he was leaving on his own accord, not because of Brash's threat. Then he meandered over to a table with a pair of whitewater rafting guides and their girlfriends. Both guides were young, blonde and muscular. One wore a gold earring. Both girls had multiple piercings. The guides ran the Kennebec River gorge below Indian Pond, but their girlfriends lived and worked in Greenville. The guides kept jet skis above the dam at Harris Station, and some evenings would scoot up Indian Pond to where the East Outlet emptied in, and where their friend Spike Jackson took his drift-boat out. They'd park their jet skis and hitch a ride into town with Spike, feeling cooler and more chic, more cowboy, than if they'd come by car.

Spike sat down with his customary theatrical flourish: he spun the chair around, straddled the seat like a saddle, draped his arms and upper body over the bent-wood back. He said something that made the others at the table laugh and look over at Whitcomb and Larue.

"What a wus," Brash said.

"I wouldn't call him that," said Conrad. "He's a lot of other things, but not that."

"I wasn't calling *him* that."

Larue sighed. "Look, I know it's hard, but try and remember, we're businessmen, OK? At least part of the time we are, and bar fights are not part of our overall business strategy, at least not as I envision it. And I feel certain that Murl would side with me on this one." Murl, even in absentia, was often called upon to mediate their disputes.

Brash stared cold-eyed at his best friend and said, "We *have* got to stop that guy."

"Yeah, yeah, I know, but not like that." Larue tapped a forefinger to his temple. "We'll use our heads."

"Just like last year, hunh?"

"Don't remind me."

The idea of using store-bought trout to trick Jackson had come to them in a weak, Murl-less moment, their judgement impaired by alcohol and hard feelings. Spike had been crowding them worse than usual on the Outlet, anchoring in the Beach Pool just outside their casting range. Aside from the breach of etiquette, his driftboat was so plastered with logos and decals—it looked like a boat sired by Nascar—that it offended their senses. "The state of Maine has a law against billboards!" Brash shouted, but Spike was anchored by a riffle and couldn't hear him, or pretended he couldn't. The noise of the riffle also meant that Spike had to speak loudly to his clients to be heard above the noise. Sound carries over water, and from shore Brash and Conrad could hear every word he said, which was, in essence, that his clients were lucky to be fishing so much better water than "those poor fellows over there," meaning Conrad and Brash.

"Can you believe that? He's calling us 'poor fellows,'" Conrad said. "We ought to sue him."

"Or kick his ass."

"I got a better idea," Conrad said. It had come to him like a vision.

That same afternoon they drove down to Waterville, where there was a little roadside store, Horton's Market, that sold fresh local produce, live lobster and live farm raised brook and rainbow trout. Conrad knew from videos and magazines that rainbows jumped, and from a distance were indistinguishable from landlocked salmon.

The men's guiding instincts led them directly past the rows of cauliflower, broccoli, Brussels sprouts and peas to the concrete tank of trout. Both men leaned over gazing in wonder at the lovely fish, finning lazily in the circulating current. "Look at those beauties," Brash said.

"They'll do for stunt doubles," Larue said. Otherwise they were little too fat and un-athletic looking for his tastes.

"I bet that one brook trout would go three pounds," Brash said.

"Can I help you gentlemen?" a woman asked.

Brash couldn't take his eyes off the fish, but the woman's voice had a stronger effect on Conrad, and he turned to see the young, pretty brunette in jeans and tee shirt with writing across the front, but the letters were distorted by her chest into, "hRon's mRet," which didn't make any sense. So he leaned down to get a better look, and the clerk smiled—she had a beautiful smile—and pulled her shirt out so that all the letters could be easily read. "Horton's Market," she said. "Same as the sign outside," she added.

"Right," Larue said. "And you would be?"

"Rona Horton."

"'Rona,'" Larue said, as if tasting her name. "I like that. We'd like eight of your largest rainbows."

"And those two big brook trout," Brash added without even turning around. He simply could not take his eyes off those fish.

"We don't really need brook trout," Conrad said.

"I *want* those two brook trout," Brash said.

"Ok, Ok."

The young woman began collecting the fish with a short handled net. When she leaned across the tank for the big brookie, her shirt-tail came untucked, revealing a slice of white skin, thin as a melon rind. Conrad felt his knees buckle slightly. There'd been no woman in his life since his divorce, which left him vulnerable to sudden, unexpected surges of hormones and emotion.

"Do you fish?" he asked, struggling for composure.

"Not really," she said, continuing her work.

"What does that mean 'not really?'"

She dropped the big brook trout into the cooler of water. "My boyfriend fishes," she said. "Sometimes I go with him."

Soon they had their fish and moved to the register to weigh them and calculate the bill. "How serious a boyfriend?" Conrad asked.

The lady lifted her left hand to display a very large engagement ring.

"Whoa! That looks pretty serious," Conrad said. "So, when's the happy day?"

"We haven't actually set a date," the girl said.

"Aha, so there's hope," he said.

She laughed—it had been a long boring day, and these guys seemed harmless—and she shook her head to indicate that no, there was not still hope, for him or his buddy. Larue looked crestfallen.

"What kind of fishing does your boyfriend do?" Brash asked, very business-like.

"I beg your pardon?" the girl said.

"Your boyfriend, is he a fly-fisherman?"

"No, not with flies," she said. "The other kind. What do you call it?"

"Doesn't matter," Brash said. Then to Conrad, "It wouldn't have worked anyway." He sounded like Conrad's chaperone.

"Nah," Larue said shaking his head. "'Irreconcilable differences.' We're fly-fishing guides," he added proudly.

"You guys are too much," the girl said. The she rang them up and took their money.

"However, "Larue continued, reaching into his wallet as he spoke, "if you, or he, should have a change of heart and care to take up the fine art of angling with the fly, let me leave you this." He laid the latest version of his business card on the counter as if displaying the final ace to a Royal straight.

>Brash-Con Guide Service, Master Guides
>The Total Maine Fly-Fishing Experience
>Featuring Super Gourmet Shore Lunches
>1-87X-FLI-FISH

Eyeing the card and then the men and then the card again with growing amusement—the carnival was in town—her smile broadened. "What exactly is the 'The Total Maine Fly-Fishing Experience?'"

"Good question," Conrad said. "You'd make an excellent student. See, we specialize in novice fly-fishermen and women. We start with a seminar on Maine fly-fishing history, then tackle, casting technique, knot tying, even some basic fly-tying instruction. It's pretty much all inclusive."

"And a gourmet shore lunch," Brash added.

"Any actual fishing involved?" the lady asked.

With that question, she had fingered their weak spot, not that you would've known from Conrad, who, without missing a beat, said, "Absolutely. In fact, we pretty much guarantee you'll catch something your first time out. And often on a fly you've tied yourself. Can't beat that."

"Not always a trout," Brash said under his breath.

Conrad cut him a quick look. When it came to business, Brash wasn't supposed to talk. "There's no way we can guarantee species," Conrad said. "You tie a good fly, no telling what'll come after it. River's full of fish."

"Well, if I or my significant other decides to take up fly-fishing, you'll be the first to know," Rona said so softly and with such a smile that it made Conrad forget his change, but Brash collected it for him, every penny.

Brash had jury-rigged an aerated live well that fit into the trunk of his "fish car," a beat up, rusted out Chevy Caprice. When Conrad had asked him how he knew how to do it, Brash hemmed and hawed and said, "Aw shucks," so convincingly that Conrad mistook his reticence for modesty. There was a lot he didn't know about Brash's past, wasn't sure he wanted to know, and he'd long ago decided that the secret to their relationship lay in their complementary skills and offsetting dispositions—an intricate arrangement of checks and balances.

Their plan was to be fishing Beach Pool early the next morning, where a cooler would not seem suspicious. They knew from Murl, who'd hacked his website, that Spike had a party booked for the next morning. Spike loved the Beach Pool; who didn't? It was prime water. When they saw Spike coming, they would each hook on big rainbows, which they'd be fighting when Spike arrived. They'd make a big fuss landing their fish, shouting back and forth, exaggerating the size—"Twenty inches!"—talking loud enough to be overheard even in fast water. They'd pretend they had taken them on tiny dries—"a #22 blue-winged olive!"—which would further reduce Spike's chance of success. Not leaving much to chance, they would already have stoned the whole pool long before Spike arrived, thereby traumatizing every fish, guaranteeing his failure. When Spike was fussing with his clients, Brash and Conrad would hook on fresh fish. "Boy this wade fishing is the best!" one would say. "Yeah, I'd hate to be stuck out in that cramped old boat," the other would reply. "Yeah, that must be awful."

Riding up the road with their store bought fish, the two men had so much fun anticipating and planning, revising and improving their lines, even imagining Spike's clients' reactions—"Who are those guys? Maybe we should've booked them."—that they started laughing so hard, and hooting and hollering so loudly that they didn't even hear the siren until the state trooper's rack of flashing blue lights totally filled the rear view mirror. Even in the side mirrors that was all they could see, blinding blue lights.

"Shit," Brash said. "Double shit. I wasn't speeding, was I?"

"I don't think so." There was no way to know for sure, because the speedometer hadn't worked for years.

After sitting in his car a while talking on the radio, the trooper came to the driver's side window. He had an erect military bearing, drill sergeant hat, shaved head. "Do you know why I pulled you over?"

"Tail light out?" Brash asked hopefully.

Trooper shook his head. "You were driving in an erratic fashion and over the posted limit. Also there appeared to be a lot of motion in the front seat."

They explained how they had been laughing and pantomiming how they were going to play a practical joke on a friend. The trooper asked them to step out of the car and take a sobriety test. They happily complied and sailed through it. Then the trooper asked if Brash would mind opening the trunk, and Brash asked, "What for?"

"I need to check for contraband."

"You mean drugs and such? We got no drugs, we don't *do* drugs," he said, his voice higher pitched than usual.

"Mr. Whitcomb," the officer began in a voice that sent a chill through both men, "according to our records, you have a prior conviction for 'Felonious Transplantation of live fish.'"

Brash realized then that they'd run his plates. "That was a long time ago, officer. I've learned my lesson. That's not to say you won't find fish in our trunk, but I can assure you that they're not for transplantation."

Brash tossed the officer the keys, and both men followed the officer around to the rear. Conrad began talking rapidly. "Officer, we're professional fishing guides, Master Maine Guides. Here, take a card." The officer took the card. "See that bumper sticker," Conrad said. "Trout Unlimited, Protecting Cold Water Fisheries. "That's us.

That's what we're all about, 'Protecting and Conserving.' We're the good guys." Which was not to say that either of them actually belonged to Trout Unlimited—too expensive—but they did genuinely support the group's principles.

The trooper opened first the trunk, then the cooler. Not being a fisherman, he wasn't quite sure what he'd found, though it appeared to be two species of fish, and he was pretty sure it was a crime.

"We got these fish at a local market in Waterville. We got them for food," Conrad said. "Horton's Market. You can check with the lady. Her name is Rona, nice looking woman. She'll remember us, I guarantee. We weren't going transplant those. We were going to feed'em to our clients. A shore lunch."

"Shore lunch?" the officer said. Even non-fishermen knew the rich tradition of the shore lunch, nearly as famous as a Maine lobster feast. "I thought the idea of the shore lunch was that you cooked fish you caught yourself. I thought that was kind of the point."

Conrad shook his head. "Those days are long gone," he said, feeling better. The man wanted to talk about shore lunches; the crisis might have passed. "See, nowadays most sports don't want you killing any fish. It's all catch and release. I'm not against it. It's a good thing. But people still want a shore lunch."

"'Gourmet' shore lunch," Brash chimed in.

"He's right. These flatlanders, you know how they are. They want fancy and authentic. Some want one; some want the other. That's why we got two species of trout. Got to satisfy the customer."

"Customer's always right." Brash said, like a backup singer. They were clicking now.

The trooper was still puzzled and skeptical. "If these fish were iced down, I might be more inclined to believe you. But these fish are alive."

"To keep'em fresh," Conrad said. "If it was just one meal, we would've iced them down. But that's a two week supply. We keep'em alive until the night before. Then we sacrifice them and dress them for our sports. Make'em look real nice, you know?"

"May I keep this card?" the officer inquired.

"Absolutely, it's for you. Here take a couple more. Word of mouth, that's where we get our business."

"Word of mouth," Brash echoed.

The trooper returned to his car and radio. Brash and Conrad stood dejectedly as a stream of vehicles—logging trucks, pickups carrying canoes—straggled by, heading to Moosehead, the nosey drivers slowing as they passed, curious passengers craning their necks.

"A prior conviction!" Conrad hissed. "You never told me that."

"Must have slipped my mind."

"Where's the trust? I feel betrayed."

"OK, you wanna know why I never told you? I'll tell you why. It was *bass* I was moving. Smallmouth bass! OK, Happy now?"

"You were transplanting *bass*?"

"It was a long time ago. I didn't know any better."

"*Bass!*" Larue repeated. That was worse than the crime; that was a lapse of standards; in fly-fishing circles it was a sign of low morals.

When the trooper returned, he said, "OK, here's the situation. I'm not writing you up for the erratic driving. I'm just giving you a warning."

"Well, that's very decent of you," Conrad said, "and, believe me, we appreciate it."

"Yes we do," Brash added. "A lot of people, less professional than yourself…"

"And as far as the fish go, well, that's not exactly my bailiwick. So I'm going to let the wardens handle that."

"Oh God, please don't," Brash cried. The state police were professional, dispassionate; even when they ticketed you, they seemed to feel bad about it, whereas the game wardens looked disappointed if they hadn't caught you breaking a law. "They're like Gestapo." Plus the rules on transporting fish were stricter now. He'd be ruined. Brash had a complete nervous breakdown on the spot. He ran around in circles bemoaning his fate, his hands raised first to the heavens, then to the officer, begging for mercy. How would he support his family? There were mouths to feed? And so on and so forth to the point that his theatrics carried him out into the highway, distracting the trooper. A fatality while in police custody was no laughing matter. Troopers had been reprimanded, even sued.

Conrad seized the opportunity and slid a couple of feet to his right, and opened the spigot to the cooler. Water trickled into the trunk and, through an array rust holes—the bottom was like a colander—onto the dusty shoulder of the road. Luckily there had been a drought; the ground was parched. Conrad casually kicked dirt over the growing puddle. Meanwhile Brash's lamentation had reached operatic proportions: he was on his knees in the travel lane, blocking a line of traffic, begging and pleading. The officer wanted to call for backup, but he couldn't abandon Brash in the road, and Brash wasn't budging.

Finally the trooper told him. "If you keep on like this, sir, I will be forced to restrain you. For your own good."

"Go ahead," Brash moaned. "Cuff me, shoot me, I don't care. All for trying to provide a quality shore lunch for my clients. I'm a sacrificial lamb." Much of his performance was from the heart; his life had not been easy—a southerner transplanted to New England. Often misunderstood and shunned because of his 'funny' way of speaking. Never to be fully accepted as a 'Mainer.' He drew on the many difficult experiences in his past—failed relationships, estranged family—and he made up a few more, and somewhere in his wailing he lost track of which was which, made up or remembered. What did it matter? His anguish was real.

Meanwhile, the trout were in their death throes, making quite a racket, but nothing compared to Brash. By the time Brash quieted down, finally without the need for cuffs, the fish had also. And by the time the warden arrived, the fish were dead. There was no law against transporting dead fish. The trooper, who by then had had a belly-full of Brash and Conrad, wasted no time exiting the scene, and was long gone when the fish carcasses were discovered.

"He told me the fish were *alive*," the warden said.

"The man is not a fisherman," Conrad explained. "He probably didn't know. He couldn't even recognize a rainbow trout. Imagine that." And imagine what a lousy witness that trooper would make in court.

"We tried to tell him, they're for food," Brash said. "But you know how they are. He didn't believe us."

"He didn't believe us when we told him we were sober either," Conrad said. "Sad day for America when you're guilty until proven innocent."

"What's all this water on the ground," the warden asked.

"Ice melted," Conrad said. "I guess he left the cooler open."

"Right warm out," Brash said. And indeed his performance had left him drenched with perspiration.

"Shit," the warden said. But his anger was more directed towards the incompetence of the state trooper than at these two. He went back to his vehicle, talked for a while on the radio, stormed back to the scene of the crime, glared at the two men.

"He swears they were alive. He says there wasn't any ice."

"I cannot believe he said that," Conrad said.

"His word against ours," Brash added. "'Two against one.'" And how reliable in court would a man be who couldn't tell a rainbow from a brookie? "It was his crime scene," Brash added unnecessarily, but he was having fun now. "If he couldn't secure it, it's not our fault. Not that we're acknowledging that there *was* a crime."

The warden knew a losing hand when he held one. "We'll be watching you boys," he said meanly before departing in a flurry of dust and flying gravel.

Later, riding slowly up the road, having thoroughly weighed and analyzed the situation, Conrad had to tip his hat to his buddy. "You did good back there. That was quite a performance, if I do say so."

"You didn't do so bad yourself. You read my mind."

"I guess that's what makes it work," Larue said. "When it does work."

True, their plan to fix Spike had been foiled, and half the fish went bad, but somehow, at the moment, both men felt triumphant.

2

"Geezer guides" was the phrase Spike Jackson used to get the first laugh from his friends at the other table. "Old codgers" got the second. But Spike said it with sadness as well as anger, because in some ways he felt bad for the older guides. There was less than twenty years age difference between Spike and them, but in those less than twenty years, the fishing world had changed.

Spike had seen the fly-fishing future in Montana. It was crowded and competitive. Fly-fishing had gone global. Maine guides didn't compete simply among themselves. Larue and Whitcomb were the least of Spike's worries. His competition could come from anywhere. From Montana and Idaho, from Alaska or the Cayman Islands, from Russia and the Caribbean. From Christmas Island, New Zealand or from Africa! Wherever there was water, fly-fishermen would find it. It was an addiction, though a healthful one, and men like Spike Jackson were the suppliers. They fed the dreams and stoked the fires, and fought for the privilege of doing it. And, of course, for the money.

More than once Spike had offered to assist Whitcomb and Larue "transition" into the future: he offered software, data bases and research tools, advice and consultation. He admired these older guides. Through them and their contemporaries, he could trace his own history back to Carrie Stevens and Fly-Rod Crosby, and, with a little imagination, as far back as Thoreau. But every overture he'd made to Larue and Whitcomb, however sincere and respectfully tendered, was met with rude resistance, derision, ridicule, even, in the case of Whitcomb, threats of physical violence. So be it. If the role were forced upon him, Spike would *be* the agent of their obsolescence, however reluctantly. Sooner or later someone was going to be. It might as well be him.

Murl was in his lawn chair reading the latest issue of *Fly Rod* by lantern light, when his two friends arrived back at their summer quarters, a camp-site on the Beach Pool of the East Outlet of the Kennebec, just below Moosehead Lake, less than a mile from the road, but beyond all sight and sound of the highway. Murl's small tent and his buddies' larger wall tent were backed against a tall stand of spruce and fir. Nearer the river a scraggly mix of white birch, maple and alder poked up among boulders, and across the river, a forest of mixed softwood stretched all the way to Greenville.

"You know what I like about blackflies?" Murl asked his friends as they joined him. "They don't bite at night. They keep banker's hours, just like me." Murl was a day-trader, hence his nickname, originally Merrill, for the brokerage firm. His real name was Tom, and he kept an apartment in town, his office, but he spent his nights beside the river with his friends.

"You don't even care that they're fish food?" Brash asked accusingly. "Blackfly larvae feed baby trout, but why would you care about that?" His run-in with Spike Jackson had left him feisty.

"Yeah, well, that too, of course. That goes without saying." Murl said.

"You're pretty mellow for a guy who didn't even bother joining his friends for a beer at the Toad," Brash said.

"You'd be mellow too if you'd made nine hundred dollars today," Murl said. "Hell, if you'd made ten dollars."

"Yeah, you make nine hundred today and lose a thousand tomorrow," Brash said. "I don't get it."

"Catch and release investing," Murl said. "What's not to understand?" Murl had long since given up trying to explain the thrill of day-trading to his friends.

Murl was taller than Brash, but shorter than Conrad and fleshier than either; not fat, but it was clear from his appearance that *he* at least could afford to eat. He also paid attention to his hygiene and grooming. When not wearing a fishing cap, he brushed his hair, sometimes parted it down the middle, and he often wore his long sleeved shirts with his collar fastened, conveying a sort of nineteenth century robber-baron/river-boat-gambler effect. But one who, of course, had a serious fly-fishing habit. However, he liked to believe that he was a bit less afflicted than his two friends, less at the mercy of the elements, that he was more disciplined, more in control, and that, for instance, a mayfly hatch wouldn't necessarily wreck his whole day. He could *chose* to stay and fish it, or, he could reel in and head off to "work," as he called it.

Brash and Conrad moved their lawn chairs closer to Murl, so they wouldn't have to shout to be heard above the murmur of the river. This night it made a lovely, unhurried sound, but other times it echoed the rushed pace down-river, the rancor and clamor of city people. For example, a heat wave—Mainers couldn't handle heat—demanded power for air conditioners, and a big release from Moosehead would send torrents of water cascading towards the turbines at Harris Station, Skowhegan and points south, rendering the East Outlet all but un-fishable. But now the river spoke softly, as if in a mother's soothing voice, the perfect flow-rate for sleeping.

"Six hundred cubic feet per second has a sweet sound to it doesn't it," Conrad said.

"That's more like six-fifty," Brash said, still in his argumentative mode. It could last for days.

"I refuse to argue," Larue said.

"Because you know I'm right."

"No, because I refuse to argue."

"Ha," Brash said, victoriously. "You're arguing now."

Murl ignored his friends' bickering, just background noise to him, same as the river itself. Much as he loved Brash and Conrad, his only real friends, they sometimes frightened him. They lived too close to the edge. The only clear difference that Murl could see between those two and, say, a pair of homeless derelicts, was the fishing. A big difference to be sure—Murl would never diminish the importance of fly-fishing—but he needed more separation than that. His apartment was very important to him—a real address with mail service, utilities, and a computer—and he *always* paid the rent on time, sometimes even before it was due.

"Hey, Murl, guess who showed up at the Toad in hip waders and a cowboy hat? Or do you not even care about this stuff any more?" Brash asked.

"Mr. Jackson?" Murl asked.

"Brash here tried to climb his tree," Conrad said. "I had to pull him off before he got his butt kicked."

"Yeah, right," Brash said, "as if that prick could do it."

"You know what I found out today?" Murl asked. "'His real name is not 'Spike.' When he was fishing out West, he was 'Jonathan' Jackson."

"Come on!"

"Naw, it's true. I Googled his ass. He wasn't 'Spike' until he came back to Maine. An image thing, I guess. Marketing."

"That is funny," Larue said rising to the edge of his chair.

"Yeah, I can't wait to use that," Brash said, rubbing his hands together.

"Well, if I were you, I would wait," said Murl. "Something like that is too good to throw away in a bar. That's valuable capital. You want to save it, invest it. Fact is, I should probably charge you for it."

"Oh, you'll get paid," Larue said, warming to the occasion.

"We're goin' to fix his wagon," Brash said. "We just haven't quite figured out how."

Murl kept flipping through *Fly Rod*, his friends chatter mingling with the river noises, until, out of the pleasing blur of sounds, Larue's voice emerged, "Anything in there worth reading?"

"Pretty much more of the same, but Gierach is always worth a look."

"It's all lies anyway," Brash said. "They'll write anything to sell a magazine."

"Nice cover," Conrad said, leaning over for a better look at a beautiful brunette cradling a luscious, buttery brown trout.

Murl handed him the magazine. "It's all yours," he said. "Hard reading in this light anyway."

Murl lay back in his lawn chair, fondly recollecting his day. Day-trading was the only thing he'd ever found that even remotely approached the excitement and mystery of fly-fishing. Some might have thought that trading stocks was the exact opposite of trout fishing—the frenzy of the trading floor, the lust for money—but Murl could've told you, it wasn't about money any more than fly-fishing was only about the fish. It was the thrill of the chase, the challenge of outsmarting the market or the trout.

Murl was a momentum player. He went with the flow. Throwing money to a rising stock wasn't too different from laying a fly out in front of a cruising trout: you had to anticipate the movement, lead it—pick a sale price—and wait until the stock or fish rose to take your offering. When your quarry hit that number, or that fly, you set the hook—you sold!—boom, click, just like that, money in your pocket. And "shorting" a stock on its way down—that was like catching a falling star, a gift from the gods.

The good part about being a day-trader, as opposed to an "investor," was that you didn't have to trouble yourself with the *Wall Street Journal*, *Barron's*, *Business Weekly*—any of that dull stuff. Murl didn't have a clue what drove the markets, and he didn't think the experts did either. He had his own way of predicting the market's opening tick, which sometimes could determine your whole day. He went by the fish. He suspected that the appetites of traders and of the fish were connected to some common underlying mystery, and that, to quote the poet, the "same green fuse" that drove the markets, drove fish.

Every trading day, rain or shine, Murl would start his morning on the Beach Pool, by far his best economic indicator. If the salmon were active and aggressively taking the fly, the market usually opened strong. If the salmon kept their mouths' shut, it was time to sell short. Simple as that. Laugh if you like, but Murl had over one hundred thousand dollars tucked away in his bank account, unbeknownst, of course, to his colleagues. That was the upside to his piscatorial stock theory. The down side was, it didn't work in winter.

One winter he tried relying on solar-lunar tables, which supposedly predicted fish activity, and Murl paid dearly. Another winter he took his summer earnings to the Caribbean, tried applying the same theory to bonefish. Another bust. Too many new variables, and he had no feel for wind, tides and weather, as they related to a salt water flat. Also beyond the lagoon, out past the line of breakers, lurked the biggest unknown of all, the deep, dark, open ocean. It unnerved him.

Conrad was intently studying *Fly Rod*, flipping back and forth, faster and faster, between the cover photo of the pretty woman and the article about her, until he'd worked himself into a state of agitation, at which point he announced, "This woman is amazing! She's a fly-fishing guide."

"Yeah, right," Brash said, glancing at the photo of the immaculately made-up, perfectly coiffed lady. "You are so gullible, dude. What is it about women that makes you so stupid?"

"You don't believe she's a guide?"

"Are you kidding? They take some model, slide her into a pair of tight waders, paint her face, hand her a trout and say, 'smile.' Why? To sell magazines to horny fools like you."

"Here, read this," Larue said, handing him the magazine. "Not only is she a guide, she runs her own fly-shop. In New Hampshire. On the Androscoggin."

Brash did not deign to look inside the magazine. "I don't need to read it. I don't doubt that's what it *says*. Of course, they're gonna *say* she's a guide. They'll say anything to lure in suckers like you. It's a big scam, dude."

Conrad was as skeptical as the next man about the media, but he didn't think a *fly-fishing* magazine would lie. This was scripture; that would be a sacrilege. "Murl, you're the expert in this area. They wouldn't lie, would they?"

Murl scrunched his face in thought. "I wouldn't think so. Be too easy to be found out. That could damage their credibility."

Brash made a dismissive noise. "And I suppose you believe the 'where-to/how-to' articles just because they label them 'non-fiction?'"

"That's different," Murl said. "People are expected to exaggerate a little bit about the fishing. But lying about that cover, that cuts right to the heart of journalistic integrity. People have lost jobs over things like that."

"There you go," said Conrad. "I rest my case."

"Look at her nails, for crying out loud," Brash said. "You ever known a guide who wore nail polish?" Conrad was silent. Brash, feeling more confident by the minute, sat up and turned sideways in his lawn chair towards Conrad. "I bet you a hundred dollars that that woman is not guide, not a real guide."

"And where would you get that kind of money?" Conrad inquired.

"From you when you lose the bet." Brash hammered the arm of his lawn chair and roared with laughter.

"I guess the only way to settle it," Murl said, "is for C-Rad to go over there and check her out."

"That's a thought," Conrad said, as if it hadn't occurred to him before.

"How else will we ever know?" Murl asked, making it sound like a question of great significance. He'd seen it coming, heard it coming—something in Conrad's voice when he spoke of the woman. And Murl understood that, from time to time, Conrad needed to make these sojourns, these expeditions in search of a woman, and if you tried to stop him, he would get restless and irritable, and eventually go anyway, and say things in anger that would make you wish you'd never opposed him in the first place. So it was better, he'd found, to be "pro-active" in these matters of the heart, same as in matters of the market, or, for that matter, fish. They all somehow worked together.

"I knew all along that's what you had in mind," Brash said. "Hell, maybe it'll be good for you. You need to have a few of your bubbles popped."

"Maybe I do," Conrad said. Then after a hesitation, "But there could be another angle to this thing too. Maybe we could use this woman—Margot is her name—to bust Spike."

"Hunh?"

"Just say for a minute that it's true that she's a guide. We book her with Spike, incognito. He starts laying all his 'how-to' lines on her, telling her she's missing strikes when she ticks a rock, correcting her casting technique, and so on and so forth, and boom! She drops her credentials on him. He'd be humiliated. And she'd let him know, or maybe we would—I haven't worked it all out—that *we* set him up. The joke would be on him. Word would get around. He'd be a laughing-stock."

Brash was not impressed. "That's the stupidest idea I've ever heard in my life."

"You got a better way to bring him down a notch?"

"Yeah, take an axe to the bottom of his damn drift-boat. Or better yet, to the top of his head."

Murl and Conrad exchanged troubled looks. They didn't know if he was kidding or not. Brash was unpredictable. They were still exploring the parameters of his personality, excavating the various layers of sweetness and rage, bitterness and sentimentality, almost afraid of what they'd find next. Both men suspected that Brash would benefit from medication, but all they had to offer was their friendship, which Brash had seized upon so avidly that sometimes Murl and Conrad felt an almost custodial responsibility. Other times being Brash's friend was more like janitorial duty, just cleaning up one of his messes after another.

"Your problem is," Conrad said, "one of your problems is, you've avoided women so long that you have forgotten their power."

"I haven't forgotten their power over you. Why do you think I'm so concerned, dude?"

"Nobody but nobody can bust your chops like a beautiful woman," Larue said with the authority that came from being the only one of the three who'd ever been married. If he'd had more confidence in his physical attractiveness, maybe Conrad would've considered a more direct approach to the woman, but his looks, per se, were not going to sweep any woman off her feet—too many funny angles in his face, and his Adam's apple was way too large. Also this Margot didn't look like the type of woman that even a better-looking man could walk right up to and put moves on. She would have to be approached more obliquely, from an angle, like a large trout in thin water. The woman was a trophy.

"Well, I'm for anything that busts Spike's chops," Brash said. "But I just don't trust your motives, and I truly despair of your future."

"I can take care of myself," said Conrad, with a sigh. He hated it when Brash got solicitous and caring. He preferred his anger. That was authentic. It was from the heart. This other business—no telling where that came from.

"If you're proposing a road trip, maybe I should go along," Brash said.

"No. N. O."

"How do I know you won't just pretend to go, and come back and tell me that I lost the bet?"

Conrad sadly shook his head. "What kind of person do you think I am?"

"You're different around women," Brash said.

"I'm going to bed," Murl said. He could tell, those two needed time alone. "I've got a big day tomorrow. Quarterly earnings are due." Not that he cared a whit about the actual earnings, but up, down or sideways, the report meant an active market, which was all Murl ever asked for—movement, action, a feeding frenzy!

"Whoopee-frigging-doo," Brash said. "Quarterly earnings! Still my beating heart!"

"That's the old spirit," Murl muttered as he retired to his tent. He'd given his buddy a fat pitch, and Brash had taken him deep. That's what friends were for.

Lying in bed, a sleeping-bag on an air mattress, Murl could barely separate the voices of his comrades from the noise of the river. They melded into a single melodious sound, rising and falling like a Gregorian chant. The words might as well have been in Latin, but their meaning was clear: harmony had been restored to the Beach Pool of the East Outlet. Life was good.

Brash and Conrad connected Murl to a larger world, a world of almost infinite possibility, a world not bounded by the usual rules, the laws of social gravity. It was liberating, invigorating and, at times, a little scary. Murl liked being a little scared. Otherwise all that separated him from being an ordinary day trader, an office worker, was the fishing. Brash and Conrad brought adventure to his life, just as he brought sanity and stability to theirs, or tried to. It was for the most part a stable arrangement, an equilateral triangle, a balance of power, needs, and fears. When things got too scary, Murl intervened.

Sometimes Murl and Conrad would think up pranks to keep Brash busy, little projects that worked like methadone to keep him off the hard stuff. Once Murl counterfeited a batch of Spike Jackson business cards on his computer. The size, texture, color, font and logo, a little fish, were perfect—it took Jackson weeks to figure it out—but the script was all Murl's:

> If your casting is perfect, and you can
> Handle criticism, call Spike Jackson.
> Until then, call 1-87X-FLI-FISH

The number was for Murl's answering machine; he handled Brash and Conrad's bookings. They planted those cards all over

Greenville—in fly shops, gas stations, grocery stores, restaurants, motels and inns—anywhere authentic Spike Jackson business cards could be found and replaced, in and a couple of places Spike hadn't thought of, such as the local massage parlor/beauty salon/tanning booth. And the cards worked too. For a while bookings increased to the point that Murl even had to take a few clients himself. By then it was getting to be too much of a good thing, and none of them were really sorry when Spike discovered the fraud and confiscated the cards. Spike knew better than to press charges. "That was a good one," was all he said the next time he saw them at the Toad. They all pretended not to have any idea what he was talking about, but they were terrible liars, except for Brash. He was a pro.

Murl had considered releasing a new edition of fake cards, but Brash had bigger ideas. "Screw the cards," he said, handing Murl a crisp twenty dollar bill. "Make some of these."

Their favorite diversionary therapy, one they all looked forward to, was their annual October fishing trip on the Kennebago River. The beauty of it was that the Kennebago officially closed in September. October fishing was illegal, which naturally appealed to Brash. In early October the fishing was wonderful, the foliage was beautiful, the weather was usually mild, and they had the river to themselves. Gone were the hordes of out-of-staters, the Orvis-clad crowds that camped out at Steep Bank or John's Pond Pool and who never condescended to hire a guide, because—who needed guides?—the sporting camp used river maps as place mats! And blazed trails to best pools. Where was the challenge in that?

The threesome always went disguised as bird hunters; they wore brush-coats and blaze-orange caps, and rugged canvas-fronted, briar-proof hunting pants. Each man carried his fly-rod in a leather gun case, along with the shotgun to splint the rod and protect it from injury. Sometimes they'd even borrow a Brittany Spaniel from a friend of Conrad's ex-wife's cousin, but as time passed, that degree of subterfuge was deemed by Brash "excessive." "Takes the sport the right out of it," he said. Without at least the threat of apprehension, where was the thrill? "In the fishing?" Murl suggested, but he knew better. Brash needed the adrenaline rush that sometimes even good fishing couldn't supply. And what harm was done? They released each and every fish they caught, and, unlike a lot of so called sportsmen, they knew *how* to release fish without causing harm.

If the fishing ever got boring, Murl and Conrad would have to come up with other ways to satisfy Brash's needs. Sometimes, at the sound of a passing logging truck, they'd drop to the ground, pretending that they recognized the engine knock to be that of the warden's pickup. A low flying plane doing fire patrol would send them scrambling for the bushes, giggling and laughing like mischievous schoolboys. The trick was to keep Brash feeling that he was living on the edge, that his renegade credentials were intact. If the wardens could have seen just how gently Brash handled fish, how carefully and lovingly he resuscitated each salmon before releasing it, they might have had to revise their whole concept of who Brash Whitcomb really was. And once a warden almost got the chance.

The three of them had just finished up in a mid-river pool that they called "Hidden" (but you wouldn't find that name on any place mat). They'd cased their rods, and climbed onto the gravel road, and were beginning the long trek back to their vehicle, when they heard a truck. Instinctively Murl and Conrad scrambled off the road and hunkered in the brush, but Brash refused to budge. "Come on, you fool," they whispered loudly, to no avail. Brash merely stepped aside to let the truck pass, but instead it pulled over. This time it really was a warden. Knowing Brash's feelings about wardens, Murl and Conrad braced themselves for the worst—angry words or fisticuffs—but all they heard was Brash and the warden chatting amiably about the lovely weather and the scarcity of game. "It'll be better when the leaves drop," the warden said.

"Has to be," said Brash.

"No dog?"

"He's off in there somewhere," Brash said, nodding towards the river. "Hardheaded rascal, dudn't mind worth a damn."

"I had one of those once."

Murl and Conrad couldn't catch every word, but what struck them was how congenial and accommodating their friend was. It was the nicest they'd ever heard Brash speak to anyone, even his so-called friends. He seemed to be enjoying himself, and sounded perfectly sincere about that dog, and they hadn't brought a dog in two years! At one point Brash even blew the whistle that he still wore around his neck as part of his disguise and called the dog's name. "Red! Come in here! Hunt close!" Then to the warden he said, "Darn thing."

The warden just shook his head in sympathy.

"He'll show up at the truck, though," Brash said. "You can count on that. He won't miss a meal. Sometimes, I swear, I'm not sure who owns who."

The warden chuckled. "Sounds like a male Brittany."

Brash nodded. "You know your dogs, awright. Course he's only part male now. I fixed that, thought it might slow him down and make him mind." He shook his head in dismay. "Hell, it sped him up. Less to worry about, I guess, you know, goin' through briars and such."

The warden chuckled some more.

This was the moment when Murl and Conrad looked at each other, shook their heads and realized that they were in the presence of, if not criminal genius, at least a very diabolical, possibly psychotic, sort of creativity. It wasn't enough for Brash to break the law and get away with it. To be fully satisfying, the crime had to be a work of art, a theatrical performance: he had fabricated a dog, given it a name and personality, then castrated it for no other reason than it made a better story. Because plenty of people hunted partridge without dogs. And Brash was so calm and convincing that later both Murl and Conrad admitted at that point they'd asked themselves, "Did we bring a dog?"

And most impressive, Brash was not irritable; he seemed to relish the conversational opportunity. He even volunteered his license—a "Super-sport" license, the most expensive kind. He was proud to show his license; it was one of his props. Even Murl and Conrad didn't buy a Super-sport." They carried the cheapest license they could buy. IF&W wasn't a charity.

Then Brash opened his coat to show the warden his empty game bag. The warden didn't bother checking the gun-case, even though Brash offered.

When Murl and Conrad heard the warden's truck pull off, they shook their heads, breathed a collective sigh of relief, and clambered up onto the roadway.

"You crazy fool!" Murl said. "That was unnecessary. That was over the top."

"You damn near gave us heart attacks," Larue said.

"What?" Brash asked innocently. "Is there a law against walking on a road with a fishing rod?"

That wasn't the point. They might beat that rap, but they didn't want their "modus operandi" revealed.

"'Modus operandi?'" Brash asked. "What are you talking about? My little boy put that rod in there. He's five and thinks it's funny to hide his daddy's things."

"Yeah, and the little brat put one in mine and Conrad's too."

"Might have," Brash said without hesitation. Then he explained how hard the last year had been on his boy—his name was Ralph—since the boy's mother died. "Brain cancer," he said with convincing sadness. He started to elaborate on her "courageous battle," and sounded almost sorry that the warden hadn't found the rod, because Brash had been deprived of the opportunity of describing her struggle.

Finally Conrad said, "Shut up, dude. You're creeping me out."

Brash shook his head and spoke to them as if addressing second graders. "Think about it, you simple tools. All I did was make it safer for us next time," though his tone of voice suggested that he personally did not take great pleasure in that particular fact. He had done it for them.

3

When you'd been living in a tent for a few weeks, as Conrad had, the humblest manifestations of man's ingenuity became as intriguing as museum items: a water faucet, a flush toilet, an electric light, and telephone—what a piece of magic that was! Imagine the human voice transmitted through copper wires. Rather frightening really, when he thought about it, because, "Suppose she answers?"

"Don't worry. She won't," Murl said. "Nobody answers their phone any more. You'll get a machine."

"Suppose you're wrong?"

"Hand me the phone."

"No way. I can handle it."

When Conrad, who'd been slowly circling Murl's apartment, came to the fly-tying table, his curiosity reached a new level: the length of some of these hackles boggled the mind. Imagine chickens genetically tricked into producing feathers that were so long they interfered with walking, never mind flying. Used to be that you needed high quality rooster necks to hackle a dry fly. Now you could tie down into the #20's with *saddle* hackle. "Amazing what they've done with hackle, isn't it?"

"Quit stalling, dude," Murl said. "Just call her."

And Jungle Cock, another miracle: an endangered species that yielded perfect little neck feathers, "nails," for making fake eyes, but for years the natural were illegal. So you were stuck with contraband—if and when you could get it—or plastic, readily available but esthetically offensive to man and fish alike. But now you could get farm raised Jungle Cock! He hefted and admired Murl's beautiful specimen. "It just goes to show that not everything is going to hell, don't you think? There's still some good left in life."

"Remember, at nine twenty-five, your window of opportunity slams shut. I'm logging on, call or no call," Murl said. He may have been the only day-trader in America without a cable modem, but he didn't mind. It was like fishing with a cane rod and silk line; if you knew what you were doing, you could catch fish on any tackle. Same for trading stocks. Two hours earlier a big salmon had hammered his little Grey Ghost, and Murl was in a buying mood.

"Yeah, yeah, yeah, I know."

Every time Conrad closed in on the phone all he felt was fear. Move away a little, distract himself, and he could feel the hope, a tiny larval thing no bigger than a mayfly nymph, stir inside. His fears were comparatively huge and all consuming. His fears were like a flock of swallows flitting and darting over a river during a mayfly hatch, gobbling up all the just hatched duns. Those poor little mayfly nymphs: two years under water going through an incredibly complicated metamorphosis, then a treacherous swim through trout-infested waters towards the surface, a desperate struggle to shed, the stretching and drying of the wings, still in range of foraging fish, then to spread the newly formed wings, to *fly*! Only to be plucked from the air like ripe fruit by marauding swallows, or by dragonflies, black and ravenous as pterodactyls.

"It's ten after nine," Murl said. "The clock is ticking."

Conrad came to a table of photos in cheap plastic frames. He never got tired of looking at fish pictures. He could trace the effects of aging on his face, the slight graying of his beard, its changing length, and on his eyes, from the hopeful, buoyant look of youth, to his more hesitant, unsure contemporary self. Even more troubling in some ways, the fish size was shrinking over the years. Numbers too, but you couldn't have told that from the photos. Gone were the glorious and bloody days of fishermen posing with a pole of fish strung through the gills, and gone, at least in those numbers, were the fish. Now the usual photo was one fisherman holding a single trout, just barely out of the water, immediately prior to the release, "grip and grin." Except there was one anomalous photo of the three of them, Murl, Brash and Conrad, arm in arm like Musketeers, all beaming broadly. "Who took that picture?" Conrad asked. "Or was it on a timer?"

"You don't remember?"

"Oh right. Slipped my mind." Cynthia, the then-wife, had taken the picture. One of her last official marital acts. His usual explanation for the end of the marriage was that she left him because she was jealous of his passion for fishing, as if he were having an affair. That sort of talk played well with his fishing buddies, because it implied that, even though he lost the woman, he hadn't lost his sense of values; he hadn't sold out. There was even a modicum of truth to it. How much truth he didn't know or want to know, and he didn't ask. The fact was, Cynthia fell for a fisherman, she married a fisherman, she left a fisherman. The fly-fishing was the one constant in their relationship; so it may not have been the deal-breaker, but if it wasn't, he did not care to know what was.

"OK, I'm going to call for you," Murl said.

"No! I'll do it myself."

"Then do it."

There was a line across which Conrad's pride would prevent his anxiety from shoving him. He might be afraid—he *was* afraid—but he would not be bullied by his fears. Hell, he wasn't a teenager any more. He could call a woman, sight unseen. It was easier, though, when he *was* a teenager and too naïve to fully comprehend the dangers women posed, or to worry then about the slow closing off of opportunities, female and otherwise. Not that he was in any way desperate; he wasn't. He still had some things going for him. The whole outdoor thing, for example. A lot of women, even Cynthia for a while, responded to that. Fly-fishing was sexy now, and he, Conrad Larue, was a by-god fly-fishing *guide*. "Gimme that phone," he said, snatching it from its cradle as if grabbing a six shooter.

But he was still quite relieved when he got Margot's answering machine. She had a husky, sexy voice, but Conrad had a telephone voice too, a deep manly voice, which he utilized to leave his message—he wanted to book a trip—and he left Murl's phone number and e-mail address. "But the phone is usually busy," he added, as if to imply that she would be lucky to get through.

"Now that wasn't so bad, was it?" Murl asked.

Conrad collapsed into an arm chair. "I need a beer! Or maybe a fish."

When Conrad got back to the Beach Pool, caddis-flies were hatching, and Brash was already anchored in his canoe on a favorite deep slot on the far side, leaving Conrad to wade fish a shallower run near shore. They both fished dry flies upstream on floating lines. They might have actually done better with nymphs, emergers, or—you never knew—streamers, but as a matter of principle, when fish rose, you used dries.

Soon Brash lifted his rod and gave a whoop. "*Yes, that's* what I'm talking about!" A bright silver fish went four feet into the air. Conrad tightened his lips in envy, and cast with more determination. While Brash was still playing and cursing his fish, Conrad yelled over, "What'd he take?"

"Little brown thing," Brash said.

"How little?"

"Eighteen, I think. Elk hair."

Conrad reeled in and went a size smaller, and quickly hooked a bright, beautiful fish of his own, smaller than Brash's, but a good fish, a solid sixteen inches, an acrobat, the best kind of fish; they wore themselves out in the air. The worst kind were the ones that ran down-river towards fast water. Conrad brought the fish in without bothering to net or measure it, seized the fly with his forceps and yanked it lose. The fish hung in the still water beside his legs, not even realizing it was free, then darted off, leaving Conrad inexplicably content.

It wasn't ego; it was a sense of completion, of having a place in the great scheme of things. Conrad Larue had pleased the fishing gods, the only deities he really believed in. He had met with their approval. It brought a great sense of peace and tranquility, and he felt drowsy and went into his tent and took a well earned nap. He'd stayed up late the night before, chatting, and then he slept restlessly, in fits and starts, his mind troubled by the vision of the woman, whom in the morning he would call. Now he'd done it, and he'd caught a nice fish—a full day's work by any measure.

He was awakened late in the afternoon by what sounded like a metal garbage can rolling down a flight of stairs, but was, in fact, Murl's truck clattering down the tote road into camp. Conrad felt peculiarly tranquil. He'd caught a nice fish, he'd had a nap, his sense of perspective had been restored. He walked out and confronted Murl with surprising equanimity. Even when Murl said, "You're on for next Wednesday," Conrad felt only a transitory wave of weakness.

"You missed a great caddis hatch," Conrad said. He would never really understand Murl's stock market fixation. "Brash hammered them. You probably heard."

"I *said* 'You're on for next…'"

"I heard you," Conrad said. "How'd she sound?"

"Hard to say. It was an e-mail. Here're the directions." He handed Conrad the print-out of her e-mail.

"Thanks."

Conrad returned to his cot, lay on his back reading and re-reading the directions as if they had been a profession of love and not simply a Word document. He inadvertently memorized the directions, as if they were the lines to a poem by Robert Frost, "Approaching from the North on Route #16…

Then he folded the paper, and folded it a second time as carefully as if it were a treasure map, and slid it into a Ziplock bag, which he placed inside a Tupperware container, which he inserted into his duffel bag between layers of clean underwear. Then he slid his duffel under his cot and, not ready to leave his precious billet-doux quite yet, lay a while longer, savoring the moment and the day.

For the next five days, Conrad fished hard; he fished early and late on the home pool, and the rest of his daylight hours on other sections of the East Outlet, or on the Roach, or the Kennebec below the Forks, or the Moose below Brassua. Rivers were the places to go during times of tribulation. So much of life, his life anyway, seemed like falling, like succumbing to the force of gravity. Water was to gravity as mist, smoke and fog were to the wind: they didn't explain the mystery, but they made it visible. So it was also with Conrad and women.

He was so relieved when Wednesday finally arrived that he left in the middle of the night. He wasn't sleeping anyway, and the drive was long and against the grain of the mountains and rivers. He cut over to Route #16, then up the Carrabassett, over to the Magalloway, down to Umbagog and along the Androscoggin. He was parked in front of the lady's fly-shop before the sun was up.

When Margot arrived, she found him slumped over, sleeping in the front seat of his truck. She rapped on the window. "Mr. Larue?" she asked, and he nodded. She said to come inside and have a cup of coffee, and by the time he was out of the truck, she was unlocking the shop. When he came inside, she was studying her appointment book, and opening the register. Without looking up, she motioned to a pot of coffee, already brewed. Soon her college-age male assistant arrived, and she left a few terse instructions—pending orders, etc.—said when she'd be back and good-by. With the same business-like efficiency she hurried back out to her truck and drift-boat and instructed Conrad to follow her down-river, to the takeout.

He followed her to a dirt, deeply furrowed, ramp beside a shallow pool, and parked his truck in the shade of a towering pine. Riding in her truck back up to the put-in, he had his first good look at her. She was wearing much less makeup than in the photo, no nail polish, and she hadn't bothered to cover the insect bites on her neck and right ear. Her hair was banded and pushed through the back of her beige baseball style fishing cap. She looked very business like, but, if anything, even more beautiful than her photo because now she looked real. She was wearing waist-high waders and a long sleeve light blue shirt that matched her eyes.

"You ever fished over here before?" she asked.
"Never have."
"What made you this time?"
"Things I'd read and heard about this stretch."
"Where, in magazines?"
"Newspapers, magazines, don't quite recall." He didn't like where this was going. She wasn't supposed to know yet that he'd seen that photo.

Her boat was a double ended McKenzie-style ClackaCraft, like Spike's, but not plastered with adds, just the name of her fly-shop, phone number and website. He helped her launch, and she checked his tackle and rigged him for nymph fishing with a strike indicator. "We'll start wet and see what happens," she said.

"You're the boss."

They started down-river. Conrad stood in the bow ready to cast, his back to her. She maneuvered the boat deftly, positioned it precisely; he was in the hands of a professional. Sometimes she would make suggestions—"by that rock…let it swing…"—but that was the extent of her conversation, not a single comment unrelated to the fishing. She did not compliment or criticize his casting; location of the fly was all. She was polite, not critical like some guides, and she put him onto fish—he caught a couple of nice, fifteen inch rainbows in the first hour—but of Conrad Larue, the person, she took absolutely no notice. She was oblivious. He was, it seemed, a disembodied, gender-neutral, fly-delivery system, a fishing robot. He didn't like it, even after he got the irony: the drift-boat as microcosm of his marriage, only this time with him as the neglected party. But he had not come for irony.

The sun was barely over the surrounding spruce and fir; mist still clung to the coves. The boat bobbed gently in the current, soothing and dream-like. The sunlight was filtered through spruce and fir, before it fell softly, in pieces, onto the water. As the morning wore on and small rainbow after rainbow were hooked, netted and released, the fishing became almost too routine. The river was like an assembly line: the fly-fisherman was inserted at one end; fish were attached like auto-fenders or rivets; later money would be extracted, yielding the finished product, a satisfied fly-fisherman, a reimbursed guide. It was fly-fishing as light industry.

Soon Margot anchored in a shallow eddy, looked up at him and smiled. "Ready for a break?" Before he could answer, she hopped overboard with her small cooler. From a nearby clump of alder she removed a pack with utensils and a one burner stove.

"I thought I'd heat up some water," she said. "Wouldn't you like another cup of coffee? Or tea? I'm having tea."

He said, "OK." Obviously this was the time and place she always stopped; break time at the fly-fishing factory.

The water was soon hot, and she fixed two cups of tea. He sat on a stump to which a single board had been nailed making a more comfortable seat. She sat on a flat rock across from him, her elbows propped on her knees, and she scrutinized him through steaming tea. He was now confronted by the full effect of her beauty, and it struck him like a force of nature, a strong gust of wind from which he was tipped slightly off balance.

"We've had a nice morning, don't you think?" she asked.

"Yes, very nice," he said, his tongue thick, as if mired in some viscous liquid. Like an engine on a cold morning with the wrong weight oil—his big moment, but the words would not come! Performance anxiety of the worst kind. Or second worst.

"I don't know what you're used to in Maine, but I hope you aren't disappointed. Sometimes those articles can be a little misleading." She was relaxed; she'd done her part. She'd put him on fish. The pressure was off her.

"No, this is fine," he said. "I'm not disappointed."

"This river does hold some good rainbows," she said. "Holdovers that'll run three or four pounds, but you can't count on catching those."

Margot made more tea, then offered him a homemade cookie, which he accepted. Then she sat back on her rock and studied him more closely. "Tell me something," she said finally. "What *really* made you come all the way over here to fish with me?"

He didn't like the sound of that. Now her beauty bore down on him like an interrogation lamp. But before he could answer her last question, she asked him another.

"Your home river is the East Outlet of the Kennebec, right?"

When he nodded yes, a drop of perspiration fell from his forehead into his tea.

She continued relentlessly. "I've heard that is the best landlocked salmon river in the world."

"I wouldn't necessarily say that," he said, but "necessarily" came out thick with an extra syllable.

"Better than anything we have. So why would you come here? Was it that magazine cover?" She could tell that she had hit a nerve. "I had a feeling," she said, without waiting for him to confirm or deny her suspicion. She sighed, then sagged slightly. "Sometimes I wish I'd never done that cover. It wasn't even my idea. It was a customer's. I thought it would help business. And it's done that all right," she said, dumping her tea. "But not quite like I expected. Don't get me wrong, the attention is flattering, but it's also a little, I don't know, intimidating. I feel so exposed. I've never had my picture out in public. And then to give the fly shop's address—it's just an invitation to trouble."

In the back of his mind Conrad heard his buddies laughing at him, and Brash chortling, "You are *so* busted, dude," but at least the spell which Margot's beauty had cast over him was broken, and broken also was the dam holding back the torrent of words that now spewed from Conrad, as if under great pressure: Spike, Spike, Spike, he said, spelling out his entire scheme, which he hadn't revealed sooner, he explained, because he was still "sizing her up," seeing if she had the talent and strength of character to handle this sort of "assignment." A number of other guides had come up short. He referred to Spike as a "rogue guide," who was giving "all of us" a bad name, because, yes, as she might have guessed, Conrad was a guide too. He handed her his card, but continued talking the entire time she was looking at it. It was the oldest trick in the book, distraction, prestidigitation—call it what you would; it worked like magic—draw attention to the left hand, produce a rabbit with the right: look at Spike, consider my plan, study my card, while I seduce you with the sound of my voice, murmuring in your ear like the music of a river.

Finally he stopped. Margot looked puzzled, bemused. "You're a guide?"

"You couldn't tell?"

"No offense, but actually I couldn't."

"I'm not offended," he said. "I take it as a compliment to my acting talents."

She read the card again. "'Super Gourmet Shore Lunches,' and all I served were tea and cookies."

"Tasted like a gourmet cookie to me," he said. "Super gourmet."

She shook her head. "I've had some pretty weird offers since that magazine came out, but I have to admit, this one takes the cake."

Conrad nodded; again he took it as a compliment.

"But why me?" she asked. "And what effect could I possibly have on someone like this Spike character."

"It has to be somebody he doesn't know. And, in my opinion, a woman's input would carry more weight."

She rolled her eyes, laughed, and said, "In my experience, just the opposite is true." She explained that she had gone to guide-school in Montana. She had been the only female in her class, and not one of the male guides took her seriously. "Just because I had a college education and was a woman, they thought I was an Eastern yuppie. They thought I was taking food from some poor cowboy's mouth. Never mind that half the other guides were from California."

"Well then, maybe there's something in this for you, aside from an all expense paid trip down the fabled East Outlet. I mean, Spike spent time in Montana too. He might've even been in your group."

"I'm not one to hold a grudge," she said. "But I always did want to fish that water."

"Well, there you go."

She tidied up the area and stashed her small cook stove behind some brush. Conrad helped her put the cooler into the boat. A big logging truck roared by on Route # 16, which he hadn't realized until that moment was but a few hundred yards away.

They moved down-river, fishing through the middle of the day into the early afternoon. Conrad now found himself calm and focused on the fishing. The spell was broken, he'd made his pitch, a decent presentation; the ball was in her court. Meanwhile he had a caddis hatch to attend to.

Caddis made trout careless. Fish threw themselves out of the water in pursuit of emerging insects. Fish that could at times be so tight-lipped and inscrutable were made foolish by a little bug. Later in the season more extreme examples would be the hatches of the almost microscopic *baetis* and *tricos* that brought large trout to the surface, in defiance of all metabolic and ergonomic logic. It didn't make sense. The cost/benefit ratio—energy expended versus calories consumed, never mind the risk of fisherman's hook or osprey's talons—did not compute. No biologist would endorse such behavior—fish would be reprimanded, sent to their rooms—but Conrad found fish that were prone to dietary indiscretions, fish that were victims of their own appetites, to be far more loveable, more human, than fish that were always sensible and discrete. "I do *love* this," he said, lifting his rod to another splashy take.

Margot smiled vacantly, distracted by her own thoughts. "If I did come—and I'm not saying I would—but if I did, where would I stay?"

"We could put you up," Conrad said, unhooking his fish, looking back at her.

"You have a place in Greenville?"

"Well, we do and we don't."

She anchored along a large eddy. He refurbished his fly and explained the setup at the Beach Pool. "Do you own a tent and sleeping-bag?" he asked. She did. He told her it was nice by the river, no traffic noise, and it was private, and she wouldn't have to be afraid, because there would be three men to protect her.

"But who would protect me from you?" she asked playfully.

He said nothing at first; he was fishing again. Then, "If the camp doesn't suit, there're plenty of motels. We'll cover your expense."

"I'm sure the camp will do fine," she said, adding, as if to some other, absent, audience, "I'm not a sissy. Or a yuppie."

"If you did come, and I'm not assuming anything, but you would have to be, ahmm, very discrete on your questionaire."

"Questionaire?"

"Spike makes every client complete a six page questionaire before they go. He keeps a computerized file. You wouldn't believe all the crap he asks? You'd think it was a dating service."

"Like what?"

"Everything you can imagine, political preference, favorite movies, foods, books, what type of birds you like, as if, you know, he could order up a flight of eagles just that. He is rather arrogant."

"That's fascinating," she said.

"It would not be cool for you to mention that you were a professional fishing guide."

"I understand that," she said. "But suppose he saw that cover?"

"Oh, I'm sure he did, but he probably breezed right past it looking for mention of himself."

"I could change my hair, just wear it up under my hat. Guys can't tell. I'll just make sure I don't wear the same outfit as I did for the cover shoot."

They fished a while in silence; the fishing had slowed. "I keep a client list," she said at one point. "I even keep it on my computer. But I never thought of a questionaire."

"What normal person would?"

"Six pages! Wow."

"This could be a very educational experience for you."

"I have *always* wanted to fish that water," she said with something akin to lust.

What was supposed to have a been a half day trip did not conclude until four o'clock. After securing the boat, they rode in Conrad's truck to retrieve her rig. The truck cab was cluttered with discarded food wrappers, a soda can, clothes and fishing gear, but now it was flooded with Margot's intoxicating aromas—hair spray and perspiration; he couldn't place them all—but he drove very slowly, practically creeping up the road, prolonging the intimate moment, until, abruptly, she rolled down her window and the atmospherics dissipated just like that.

"You know," he began as if he hadn't been planning this moment for the last two hours, "by the time we come back down with your rig and load the boat, it'll be getting close to supper time. I was thinking of getting a bite to eat before heading back. Wondering if maybe you might care to join me?"

She fidgeted in her seat. "That's OK," she said. "I can handle the boat alone. And you've got a long ways to go."

"Well, I assure you that I am not going anywhere until we get your boat loaded."

"That's noble of you, but…"

"What kind of person do you take me for?" he added, sitting as tall in the seat as the broken springs would allow.

"A gentleman, obviously, but my truck has a power-winch."

"Speaking of powerful wenches," he said making a little joke, and she laughed as if maybe she'd heard it before, as if maybe she'd heard it all before.

"The truth is," she began delicately, "as a rule, I don't socialize with my clients." That was a lie. She socialized with plenty of them, but—this was the rule—she tried to avoid the marginal types. She favored the ones with paying jobs, and, though she had no formal policy on people living in tents—she'd never needed a policy—she thought they would probably fall into the "marginal" category.

"Who said anything about 'socializing?'" Conrad asked, making it sound dirty, as in "socialism." "I was merely offering to buy you dinner, so as I wouldn't have to eat alone. It wasn't my intention to compromise your business principles." His righteous indignation carried more weight than it might ordinarily have, because he hadn't paid her yet, and they both understood that her tip, as much as twenty five percent of her fee, hung in the balance.

"But you've had a long day. I'd think you'd be in a hurry to get back. Usually, when my clients drop me off, that's it."

"Fine then. I didn't mean to impose." Indignation had given way to an air of injured nobility. The woman had no idea of the subtle gradations of his personality. She would learn, there was more to Conrad Larue than fishing. He was 'vast and contained multitudes.' It occurred to him that he might even have been a bit too complex for her, too nuanced and layered.

Something about his ridiculous posturing and the way he jutted his chin made Margot smile and turn her head to the side as if studying the passing river, now close beside the road. "Look," she said finally, "after you drop me off, I'm going back to load my boat, and stow the gear. And then what I usually do is go over to this little restaurant near Errol—nothing fancy, just home cooked food—and get a salad and a sandwich or a bowl of soup. If you want to follow me over there," she said, lifting her hands in resignation, "you're welcome to join me."

4

Brash Whitcomb was having a very bad day and was even more disgruntled than usual. A borderline insomniac to begin with, he had been sleeping lightly, when his tent-mate arose in the middle of the night and, with a great rattling of gear and the roar of a poorly muffled truck, departed for New Hampshire. Why Conrad had to leave in the middle of the night was a great mystery. In fact, why he had to leave at all was a mystery, other than that, once again, he had fallen under the spell of a woman.

For the next couple of hours Brash tossed and turned on his army cot trying to get comfortable, and trying not to think of Conrad and his foolhardy scheme. Then, still in the middle of the night, loosely defined, birds began to caw, chirp and tweeter most annoyingly. "Damn!" Brash said, pulling the sleeping-bag over his head.

June in Maine offered an unnatural amount of daylight. Actual darkness in mid-June was maybe six and a half hours. All the rest was day. Once, as a part of a so-called friend's evil scheme, Brash had been lured into a trip to Alaska, where supposedly he would work as guide and all-around handyman, though his real intention was to fish. When he considered the fishing, the "land of the midnight sun" sounded like a good thing, but when mid-night actually arrived and a man needed sleep, the sun was still glaring evilly, like the lone eye of a diabolical Cyclops. For his own safety, and for the safety of those around him, Brash was airlifted out. Because when Brash lost sleep, his temper became so short as to be un-measurable. He got mean.

To wit, the very day of Conrad's departure, Brash stoned Spike Jackson's drift-boat, and with good reason: after an inordinate amount of Nyquil, three beers, and a vigorous session of supposedly tranquilizing exercise, Brash had finally dozed off in his lawn chair about mid-morning. He'd almost dozed off earlier, but kept himself awake until Murl left. Then Brash had another beer and sat in his lawn chair, swatting flies until he began to feel very drowsy.

Rather than return to the cot, the scene of his last unsuccessful sleep attempt, he slathered himself with more DEET and fell asleep in the sunshine, amidst a background noise of flowing water and frustrated blackflies droning and humming around his head.

Then came shouting and commotion, as one of Spike Jackson's loud sports fought a frisky salmon from Spike's boat, anchored not a hundred feet from where Brash slept. He woke up in a fury and ran to the water's edge, screaming and cursing. Spike as usual cupped a hand to his ear, pointed to the riffles, and shook his head, as if to say, "Sorry, can't hear a word you're saying."

For Brash, reaching for rocks instead of his handgun represented a major act of self restraint. However, the shoulder of his throwing arm was so inflamed from excessive casting that every stone fell short, throwing up sizeable geysers of water, like an artillery barrage called in with the wrong coordinates. His point, however, was made, and Spike, shaking his head and making an obscene gesture, quickly weighed anchor and rowed off down-river, while his sports—a couple from New Jersey on their first trip to Maine—looked on in absolute horror, with, Brash figured, visions of the movie *Deliverance*—buggery and murder!—likely to disturb *their* sleep for a good long while. The symmetry of it was quite satisfying, and the sight of Spike Jackson, the very embodiment of Brash's insomnia, beating a hasty retreat down-river, worked like a soporific: Brash had defeated insomnia, had conquered sleeplessness, literally driven it away. He went inside his tent, collapsed onto his cot and slept soundly until after five, when Murl returned from "work."

"How was your day, dear?" Murl inquired of Brash, who stood before his tent stretching and yawning.

Brash felt surprisingly refreshed. "All in all it wasn't a bad day," he said.

Then like an old married couple, they opened beers, sat in their lawn chairs surveying their stretch of river and discussed their days, which in Murl's case included a couple of "exquisitely timed" trades. "Bought on the upslope, sold at the peak. Doesn't get much better than that," he said, lifting his beer in a solo toast to the moment. In fact, he'd only made about fifty bucks all day, but the pleasure of that trade far exceeded its dollar value. Of course, he couldn't expect a man of Brash's sensibility to fully appreciate the moment. And Brash didn't.

He brushed it aside and said, "I had a rather satisfying moment myself, with our buddy Spike." As he shared the events of his day, he became increasingly animated, fleshing out his tale with hand gestures and a grotesque array of facial expressions. "I thought the woman would faint and fall overboard," Spike howled.

Murl sat on the edge of his chair, alarmed. "You did what?"

"I threw a couple of rocks. I didn't hit them. Just made a statement."

"Jesus!" Murl said. "I can't even leave you alone for one day."

"I should've known you'd react like that, you, you…frigging *stockbroker*, you *capitalist*." It was the worst he could think to call him. "What do you know? Too bad C-Rad's not here. He'd see the humor. It was funny as hell." He laughed some more just recalling the incident.

"It's not funny! Do you understand?" Murl's voice rose with agitation. "In this day and age, you could be charged with assault with a deadly weapon. You don't know those people! He might have been a lawyer. They might have both been lawyers!"

"'Assault'? More like freedom of speech, if you ask me. Maybe you had to be here to get the humor," Brash said. Now his feelings were hurt. He'd felt like a hero: he'd repelled the invasion. He'd expected praise. Murl was always a disappointment.

Still muttering, Murl opened another beer.

"Look on the bright side," Brash said. "Think of the story they'll have to tell back home. Their 'Adventure in the Maine Wilderness.' Christ, Spike should pay us to throw rocks and do shit like that. Like a theme park, it would liven up his trips. Especially on the slow days. I think I'll suggest it to him next time I see him." He was feeling better; this seemed like a great idea. Sometimes, as Conrad always said, visionaries had to trust their instincts, push through the opposition, ignore the nay-sayers.

"You just better hope that the next time you see him is not in court."

Brash had stopped listening to Murl's chirping. He was contemplating ways to spice up Spike's trips. A bear suit came to mind, followed quickly by, "Shit no, I'd be shot in five minutes." He was glad he hadn't said "bear suit" aloud. Murl would've crucified him, but there were other things. One bad idea didn't invalidate the whole concept.

"Sheriff will probably be down here any minute to take you in," Murl said.

"For throwing rocks? I don't think so. Hell, I didn't even hurt his fishing. The man caught a *nice* salmon right there," Brash said, pointing to the spot.

"He did? Right in front of the camp?" Murl asked in a different tone of voice. That "stockbroker" comment hurt more than he let on.

"I could've hit him with a roll cast, but I was sleeping."

"Wait a minute. Let me make sure I got this straight," said Murl. "While you were sitting here in your lawn chair, 'resting the pool,' that S.O.B. had the nerve to drop anchor in casting range."

"What do you think I've been trying to tell you, for crying out loud?"

"I thought he was just drifting through, and, for the hell of it, you'd start throwing rocks. You didn't mention the fish."

"You didn't give me a chance. You were too busy criticizing and passing judgement."

"That ballsy son of a bitch," Murl said.

"Well, yeah." That was more like it.

"That changes everything. That is entirely different. Hell, that's not assault. You were just enforcing the ethics of fly-fishing. You were acting as the river-keeper."

"Well, there you have it," Brash said.

"If it ever did come to court, every wade-fisherman in Maine would testify on your behalf."

"The question is, would you?"

"Absolutely," Murl said. "Hell, if it'd been me, I might have shot the fucker."

"Don't think it didn't cross my mind," Brash said.

Murl, more serious now—maybe he'd over-compensated—said, "*I* was just kidding about shooting him. You do understand that, don't you?"

"I don't know," Brash said, eyeing him skeptically. "You got a crazy streak in you. I better keep an eye on you."

Murl chuckled. "You didn't just make that up about the fish, did you."

"No! It was a big male, eighteen inches, maybe more. What'd you think I was so upset about?"

Murl shook his head. "That is simply unacceptable behavior."

Harmony had been restored. So accustomed was Brash to the miraculous powers of fish that it seemed perfectly plausible to him that one salmon could totally alter Murl's interpretation of the episode with the stones, could turn it a hundred eighty degrees in an instant, in about the time it took a salmon to snatch a fly and streak away.

Murl puttered about, making dinner. "You don't think we should wait for Conrad?" Brash asked.

"No telling when he'll be back."

"Half a day trip. Three and a half hour drive. He should be back *now*."

"Wait if you want. I'm eating." Murl tossed chopped-up, parboiled potatoes and raw onions into a greased fry pan, venison steak into another pan. He held Brash's steak in the air. "Your call."

"To hell with C-Rad," Brash said, and the steak hit the hot pan with a furious sizzle.

Most of their perishable food was kept at Murl's apartment, and transferred bit by bit to the camp cooler. Brash and Conrad purchased, or in some way acquired, the larder; Murl supplied electricity. The venison had been legally taken last season, tagged, butchered and frozen, along with a hind quarter of a moose—a lot of meat—that Brash had just showed up with one day. "A friend of a friend was a sub-permitee," he said, making it entirely possible that the moose meat had been legally acquired. No further explanation was requested or provided. He even gave the others clumps of mane for flies, though they didn't tie mosquitoes much any more. It was an old fashioned pattern, but it never hurt to have a supply of moose mane just in case.

There was plenty of daylight left after dinner; so Brash rigged up, launched his canoe and paddled towards his favorite deep slot on the other side. "Thanks for leaving me the water you just stoned," Murl said.

"That was ages ago," Brash shouted back. "Besides, sometimes it perks them up."

The Beach Pool offered many types of fishing situations: deep runs, riffles, slots and chutes and tough, heavy tail-water. They knew the micro-environment of each riffle and run; they knew that, for instance, it wasn't enough to send your streamer through a certain run at a certain depth, but that the cast had to end a few inches above and to the left of a submerged shelf of ledge, where, often, there would be the heavy take. Not even Spike knew that water as well as these three, and they didn't plan on giving him the opportunity to learn. They'd run him off same as they would chase marauding crows and groundhogs from a garden. "That's an idea," Brash thought as he anchored his canoe. He'd rig up a scarecrow, like a fall-figure, stuff some clothes with leaves and hay, and prop it in a lawn chair with a rifle up against it for when nobody was around to protect their water. Some days Brash was so full of good ideas that they poked out of him like the stuffing of a scarecrow.

Brash cast a nymph under a strike-indicator upstream into the slot, followed it with the tip of his rod, fingering the slack line as it floated back towards him. Brash was the only one of the three who really enjoyed upstream nymphing with a strike-indicator. "Like bobber-fishing," the others said, as if there was something wrong with bobber-fishing. He liked bobber-fishing; it's what he grew up doing, and upstream nymphing reminded him of it in a nice way, and also of dry fly fishing, because it was visual: he focused totally on the strike indicator, a tuft of red yarn, and when it stopped or sank, he struck. A very effective way of taking fish.

From a distance, Brash's casts looked identical, but each cast relocated the nymph a few inches closer to overhanging alders and underlying boulders, a painstaking, almost surgical, exploration of the run, and one that was simply not available to the bank fisherman. So it didn't matter how many people had waded through in a day; rarely was that piece of water thoroughly probed.

On his fourth cast, the strike indicator plunged down, Brash lifted and felt the live weight of a fish. Before he could say, "fish on," a sixteen-inch salmon leaped not ten feet from his canoe. On the second leap it threw the fly. No matter. "That was sweet," Brash said. And that was enough. He raised the anchor through a pulley-rig over the bow, and paddled through the heavy water back to shore. Amazing how a day that started so poorly could have such a sweet conclusion, because when that fish jumped, the sun had struck its flank from such an angle as to make it shine like chrome, then copper, an image of precious metal that imprinted itself on Brash's retina. He'd remember that one for a long time. It was better than a photo; photos faded. He wouldn't mention it to Murl for fear of being laughed at, though he suspected that Murl and Conrad kept similar albums in their minds.

"That was quick," Murl said, as Brash dragged his canoe up onto shore.

"Enough is enough." He didn't want to blur that one image with others, like a double exposure. There were days when fish overlapped fish, and those were good days too, but sometimes one was just the right number.

"What'd he take?"

"Number fourteen bead-head hare's ear."

"Very sophisticated offering," Murl said sarcastically.

"The sophistication was in the cast, shit-for-brains." Brash was *so* misunderstood; he rarely got credit for his accomplishments, but he didn't care. That was the role he had been assigned. If he played it well, if his performance pleased his friends, Brash too was pleased. He opened the final beer of the day, his ceremonial night cap. He toasted the river, and, though his friend couldn't see because he was facing the river casting, he also toasted Murl, his part-time adversary, his full-time friend.

By dark, there was still no sign of Conrad, and Brash was getting frantic. "Maybe something happened."

"I'm sure *something* happened," Murl said.

"Naw, I mean like an accident. Maybe I ought to call the state police, just to see."

"Get a grip, OK?"

"It's ten o'clock!"

Murl sighed. Brash, for all his irregularities, had this old woman side to him, the spinster aunt in a rocking chair, the neurotic worrier. "He might have gotten into fish. He might have stayed all day. He might have fished until dark…" Murl said.

"You ever kept a client overtime just because you found fish?"

"He might've fished on his own *after* he finished fishing with her. Hey, he might have even gotten lucky. He might've gotten laid!"

"It's no laughing matter. You know how he is with women. He goes all to pieces. He loses control!"

"Isn't that what you're supposed to do with women?" asked Murl. "He's a big boy. He's been married, for crying out loud. Which is more than either of us can say."

"That's what worries me. I think he's looking for that sort of thing again. Guys like you and me, we can learn, we can even get laid, without having to get married. I found out a long time ago that I wasn't fit for marriage. And I didn't have to get married to figure it out."

"Well, when it comes to relationships, you are indeed a role model. No doubt about it, you are the template to which we all aspire."

"Screw you, dude."

Brash was quiet for a few minutes. Sometimes it was impossible to conduct a serious conversation with Murl. Sometimes it seemed the man only cared about money and the stock market, not people. Brash *cared* about his friends. He wasn't ashamed to admit it. He had *feelings* for his buddies. That didn't make him gay. It made him human.

"You know what I think we ought to do?" Brash said, after further reflection.

"I'm afraid to ask."

"I think we should have an *intervention*."

He said it with such solemnity, so self-importantly, that it struck Murl as hilarious, and he choked on his beer. "You are too much," he said, when he finally cleared his airway.

"Everything's a joke to you, but I'm serious," Brash said. "I think the two of us ought to sit him down and tell him that we care about him, and that we're concerned. Because it isn't normal for a man to drive all the way to another state to see a woman that he's never even met, that he's only seen in a magazine. That is *not* normal male behavior. You'll never convince me otherwise."

"Blame yourself. You provoked him. You made that bet."

"That's not why he went, and you know it."

"You know what?" said Murl. "You missed your calling. You should have your own TV show. Dr. Brash. Or maybe just a call-in show on the radio. People could ask you questions about relationships, their love lives."

"Yeah, maybe I should."

"I wasn't serious, you ignorant…"

"But I wouldn't call it 'Dr. Brash,' or doctor anything. It was just be one experienced layman's opinion. An expert doesn't have to be a doctor. Look at Ann Landers. She wasn't a doctor."

It was close to midnight when the headlights of Conrad's truck came bouncing down the tote road, their beams climbing slowly up, down, and across the backdrop of spruce and fir beside the campsite, as he navigated his way over small boulders, slabs of ledge and around washouts large enough to disable a Saab or Audi.

After killing the engine Conrad loudly slammed the truck door to herald his return, then hitched up his jeans and swaggered over to the lawn chairs where Murl and Brash kept vigil. "Well, Mr. Whitcomb, looks like you owe me a hundred bucks."

"I'm supposed to take your word for it that she's a guide?"

"You don't have to take my word for it. You can ask her yourself. Because the woman is coming here."

"You're shitting me," Murl said.

"Nope, I landed the big one."

"Did you nail her?" Murl asked.

"What?"

"You got lucky, didn't you? You got laid."

"No!" Conrad said. "That is *not* what I meant. And please don't use that sort of language in reference to Margot or in her presence. This is a lady that we're talking about. A class act."

"You poor bastard," Brash said. Then to Murl, "What'd I tell you? Hunh? Did I warn you?"

Murl ignored him. Instead he addressed Conrad, now riffling through the cooler for a beer. "So what's the deal? Seriously. Talk."

"The deal is, the woman is coming for a visit. Here, to this very camp."

"Why?" Murl and Brash asked in unison.

"Well, motives are tricky things, particularly women's motives," Conrad said expansively, gazing into the distance, like a professor of female psychology addressing a class of undergrads. "Maybe she's coming because she wants to fish this water. She's always wanted to fish this water. On the other hand, maybe it's because she wants to help with Spike. Or," he shrugged with false modesty, "perhaps she would like to get to know yours truly, Conrad Larue, a little better. Only time will tell." At dinner with Margot he thought he'd given a good account of himself; he'd played it cool; he made a comeback. He wasn't a strong man, but he was resilient, which in the long run, was better than being strong. Once a strong man broke, he often stayed broken—he could give examples—but a resilient man bounced back.

"When's she coming?" Murl asked.

"Soon as she can book with Spike. She'll e-mail you."

Conrad looked around at the disarray of the campsite, clearly visible even in the weak lantern light, and he hated to think how much worse it would look in the morning: beer cans and bottles strewn everywhere; leftover dishes and containers of half-eaten food cluttering the upturned cable spool they used as a dinner table, dirty laundry hanging from tent ropes, a roll of toilet paper out in the open. "We need to get this place cleaned up," he said.

"Let her clean it up," Brash said.

"Don't talk like that, OK? Seriously."

"You poor lovesick bastard."

"That all you got to say?"

Then Conrad opened a beer and sat with the others and gave a brief recounting of the day. Naturally, Murl and Brash had questions about the fishing and the water. How did the river compare to the East Outlet? How hard did those rainbows fight? What flies did they favor? What sort of presentation? And finally, did this Margot woman actually know what she was doing? Conrad said that she handled the boat flawlessly and that she handled him, her sport, flawlessly. She put him on lots of fish, helped him land them, and released them expertly.

"What does she use for rods?" Brash asked.

"She carries two Sages, a four-weight with a floating line and a six-weight with a 150-grain sink-tip."

"A four-weight?" Brash said dismissively. "What the hell does she need that for?" A four-weight sounded mighty prissy to him, an affectation, as if to say, "Let's see how dainty and delicate we can be."

"For dries," said Larue.

"Anything you can do with a four-weight, you can do better with a five or a six."

"Don't mind him," Murl said. "He's had a very stressful day."

Then it was just the three of them and the sweet sound of the river at a steady six hundred CFS, the smell of damp leaves and pine needles, and the half moon rising over the river, spreading a broken pattern of silver across the riffles.

5

Conrad felt a great stirring within. For the first time in ages, he reconsidered the possibility that his two great passions—fly-fishing and women—might be united in a single entity. Since the debacle with Cindy, those feelings and that hope had lain dormant, hibernating. More like a coma. Too much pain. But now he dared to hope again.

Conrad had a theory that the secret to a lasting relationship was a shared faith. He got the idea, not from fishermen, but from Christians, whom, in his early years, he'd had ample opportunity to observe. He'd never understood the religion, but Conrad had noticed and envied the looks on the faces on the worshippers when they lifted their voices in song or lowered their heads in prayer. They seemed happy, content. Some practically glowed and none quite so radiantly as young Maribelle Weeks, who in her ruffles and pony-tail looked like an angel, but wanted nothing whatsoever to do with a heathen like Conrad Larue. Except that she prayed for him. In turn, he pretended that her prayers had been answered, that he had been converted, but even at age thirteen Maribelle was not quite that gullible. It made Conrad wish that he really could believe, or, alternatively, that he had been a better actor.

Then in his later teens a buddy introduced him to fly-fishing and changed his life. Conrad loved every part of it: tying flies, learning hatches, reading water, finding fish and enticing them to reveal themselves and take the fly. It was totally mesmerizing; hours of his time, entire weekends, were consumed by fly-fishing. One night after a crazy caddis hatch on the Cupsuptic River, Conrad caught a glimpse of his own face reflected in the water as he was releasing his umpteenth brook trout. He looked so deranged, possessed, that he hardly recognized himself. His eyes were glazed, his hat was cock-eyed, and his hair stuck out in four directions like the points of a compass. He leaned over and took a closer look, and he recognized that crazy, deliriously happy look: he had the eyes of a Christian zealot and the beatific smile of the true-believer.

But a few short years later, when he met Cindy he betrayed his faith and downplayed his love of fly-fishing. He called it—it hurt to remember—a "hobby," and no sooner had the words passed his lips than he knew he was a hypocrite. But he wanted Cindy; he needed her. From sand-colored pony-tail to her look of rural innocence, pretty, unformed, and malleable, she was a grownup version of Maribelle Weeks, with whom honesty had *not* been the best policy. So this time he lied. Yeah, he fly-fished; it was "fun." Did she like fishing? No, well, no problem. They'd find other things to do together.

It helped that they met in winter, when the rivers were rock solid and about as appealing as a corpse. When spring came, Conrad snuck out a few times on his own, but he didn't dare take Cindy until the third year of their marriage.

For their inaugural trip he naturally chose the Cupsuptic River, the site of his own conversion, his personal road to Damascus. Sadly by then the cathedral atmosphere of spruce and fir had been mutilated by a logging company that had clear-cut right down to the river's edge. To hell with the seventy-five foot buffer, they'd even dropped a few trees across the river, leaving a tangle of trunks and branches, making walking difficult, even dangerous. Also Conrad had forgotten to warn Cindy about the hordes of blackflies that hovered around your head just waiting for the DEET to wear off, at which point every exposed surface and some that weren't exposed were vulnerable to attack. Unlike mosquitoes blackflies were strong runners. A hand or wrist was just a beachhead for an assault of the entire arm. An earlobe was the gateway to an expanse of tender neck and a jungle of scalp. Blackflies chewed their ways through the skin in search of blood; the puncture site was anesthetized by the bug's saliva; so that the bite itself was relatively painless and the first indication of attack would often be a trickle of blood down an extremity, or belatedly a welt that wouldn't just itch—that was the least of it—but would hurt for days, sometimes fester and lead to cellulitis. For serious fly-fisherman, that was a small price to pay—blackflies equaled good fishing—but for Cindy, it was a day in hell.

When he got back to her, she was hysterical, and before his very eyes, her softness and malleability was exposed as an ugly form of helplessness: it was *his* fault that she had fallen and ripped her waders; *his* fault that her hands and scalp were bleeding from bites. "You bastard!" she said. "You left me here. You abandoned me!"

He *had* left her, but he thought he was doing a favor by not crowding her or over-coaching. Then he unwisely asked, "Did you catch any fish?"

At which point Cynthia collapsed in tears. "'Fish?'" she said. "'Fish?'" she asked again, laughing and crying, wiping blood from her face onto her hands, holding her blood stained hands out for him to see, as if she had been crucified by him. "And *he* wants to know if I caught fish." Her reference to him in the third person was an indication of the distance she was already placing between them, a mile marker on the roadmap to ruin, to the end of their marriage.

And yet in the long run, he was grateful to the river for revealing the error of their ways. A river was like a Rorschach; it exposed your hidden feelings. A river was truth serum; you couldn't lie to a river. A river x-rayed a relationship: showed you the underlying architecture, like it or not. But love that you discovered on a river, that love was legit; it would last. Or so Conrad fervently believed.

Margot was the first woman since Cynthia to arouse those thoughts and feelings. No wonder he panicked, when, one evening not long after the initial visit, Murl returned from his apartment with the news that Margot would be arriving Tuesday, less than five days away. That left precious little time to prepare. "This camp is a wreck," Conrad said, eyeing the mess. "It looks like a shanty-town around here." Near the river two crows pecked at chicken-scraps. "Get out of here!" he said shooing them off, gathering scraps and loose papers into a garbage bag.

"Pussy-whipped already," Brash said.

"You know, you might want to consider moving into town and staying at Murl's apartment while she's here."

"Are you shitting me?" Brash asked. "I wouldn't miss this for the world."

The next morning Conrad was up at first light, collecting litter, smoothing a place for Margot's tent, and laying out the plans for an outhouse.

"Look at it this way," he said to Brash—Murl had gone to work—"It's like when the Olympics come to town, after the show is over, the locals reap the benefits of the 'infrastructure improvements.'"

Brash tightened his face in thought. "Just don't lose your sense of humor about this deal, OK?"

"Not to worry," Conrad said, patting his butt, "It's right here in my back pocket."

"Awright then," Brash said, then headed off down-river to take a quick shot at the water before Spike came through.

Conrad moved several large rocks to make a suitable place for Margot's sleeping area. It worked out that the last flat spot was between the two tents already there, but considerably closer to his and Brash's tent than it was to Murl's. There weren't many options; they'd monopolized as much space as possible to discourage others from even thinking about camping there. Likewise, to discourage day-trippers, they'd left most of the huge potholes in the tote road untouched. But now Conrad placed a few of the larger, flatter stones removed from the sleeping area into the deeper holes, to make sure that Margot had enough clearance. A ruptured oil pan could be a real mood killer.

As Conrad went about his morning's work, he couldn't help being reminded of fixing up his and Cindy's first apartment, selecting curtains and furniture, even designating one little room for any possible addition to their "family," though in the meantime, temporarily, with Cindy's permission, Conrad would use it as his fly-tying room. Later, when things went bad, she would cite his use of the "baby's room" for fishing purposes as evidence that he never really wanted a family. Later still she would retract that cruel remark, which they both recognized as the sort of thing people said in the heat of battle, aided and abetted by bastard-lawyers, whose interests were best served by a bitter and protracted divorce. Afterwards, Conrad and Cynthia rightly aimed their anger at the lawyers—"Before they got involved there was enough money to go around!"—and forgave each other. "Irreconcilable differences." Whoever thought that one up, Conrad believed, should get a Nobel Prize for euphemisms. It was particularly handy around nosy relatives.

As for his most important project, the outhouse, Conrad believed that as with any real estate, the key was location, location, location. A woman needed privacy, and preferably a view of the river, and definitely something better to sit on than the driftwood log that the three of them used. This meant lumber. After he found the ideal spot, an elevation on a little esker with enough sand for a hole of sufficient depth, Conrad headed off to a building site in town, where some of his construction worker buddies were rebuilding a burned-out restaurant. His friends were happy to offer scrap lumber—that much less for them to remove—and even let him use their table saw, and loaned him nails and a hammer, no questions asked. It goes almost without saying that these generous souls were of Conrad's faith, fly-fishermen to a man.

For corners, he used standing saplings, two birch and two hemlock, not, of course, at right angles to each other, but that would be part of the structure's New England charm: it was a trapezoid. A thick layer of polypropylene formed the roof; no floor, of course, just the wooden pedestal with a cut out hole. The actual toilet seat, his piece de resistance, was fashioned from a pair of old canoe carrying-yokes. The curved center portions were solid oak, which he sanded and lacquered until they shone like sculpture. Set in place facing each other, they formed the perfect oval aperture for Margot's glorious derriere. The wooden door was hinged with old rubber shoe soles; its handle carved from deer antler. The overall effect was folk art and, Conrad thought, quite charming, if you went in for that sort of thing. However, leaving nothing to chance, he built a crude table of curved driftwood, on which he left the latest issues of *Fly Rod* and *Gray's Sporting Journal*, a roll of scented toilet paper, and, his finishing touch, a Moosehead Lager bottle filled with freshly picked trillium and lupine.

He had learned the hard way that flowers, especially ones you'd picked yourself, had an inexplicably huge effect on women. The angriest, most embittered woman could be softened with a bouquet of the most ordinary flowers, the names of which, you didn't even need to know. Women's weakness for all things floral cut to the central mystery of gender differences. Luckily the only part that men needed to understand was, it worked. Like gunpowder, you didn't need to understand the chemistry of volatile nitrates to shoot somebody. All you had to do was aim and pull the trigger. So it was with flowers and the enigmatic chemistry of women.

Which was why, a few days later, Conrad was waiting along Route #6 with a bouquet of wildflowers, which he held behind his back because he was embarrassed to be seen with them in public. When a truckload of his construction buddies pulled in beside him, he was almost busted. "You broke down or something? You need a ride?"

"Naw, thanks. I'm just waiting on a client," he said. She *was* a client, just not his.

"Whatcha got behind your back?"

"Get the fuck outta here."

They hadn't gotten all the way across the bridge when Margot Montgomery's maroon Toyota Tundra pulled in with a friendly toot of the horn. Quickly Conrad hopped into the front seat and handed her the flowers. "Oh my goodness," she said. "That's sweet."

Conrad had forgotten what it was like to share a truck cab with Margot and immediately felt the disorienting effect of her aromas, further sweetened by the wildflowers. He felt lightheaded and as weightless as a fish in water, felt like he was drifting—or pulled by pheromones—towards her. He steadied himself; Margot was eyeing the rear-view mirror. "What are you looking for?" he asked.

"My drift-boat. I just feel so *naked* without that boat behind me."

The word '*naked*' hit Conrad like an aphrodisiac, an additional and totally unnecessary threat to his composure.

Then she added, "I feel like an amputee, like I'm missing a limb."

That was better. It was clinical and it cleansed his palate and cleared his head. "You weren't lying about this road," she said, navigating around deep washouts and over ledge.

"Just keep one wheel up on ledge and you'll be all right," he said, as if reading from an abstruse self-help manual, written in metaphor: when you're losing traction, use four-wheel drive and keep one tire on solid ground at all times. He rolled down his window to inhale the fresh but vapid outside air. It was boring air. Breathing it was like drinking non-alcoholic beer. Sure, it replaced your fluids, but otherwise what was the point?

Brash and Murl were fishing when Conrad and Margot rode into camp. Conrad was grateful for that moment alone. Margot stood beside the truck and stretched her back and legs and arms. She was wearing the light blue cotton shirt and jeans and just enough makeup to show she was not indifferent to her appearance. Her hair was pulled back and cinched in a pony-tail. "This is gorgeous!" she said. "What a great spot!"

"Well, it's not fancy, but we call it home, at least sometimes we do."

"I should put those flowers in some water."

He filled a beer bottle from the river away from where his friends were fishing. Then he showed her the place he had smoothed for her tent, and began to unload her gear. Her tent was no more than thirty feet from his and Brash's; Murl's was across the clearing. When Margot ran off to the "ladies' room," Conrad held his breath. When she returned she was smiling. "That's quite a facility you have there, I must say. I hadn't expected anything that fancy."

Conrad shrugged modestly. "We aim to please."

"Is that a uni-sex facility or…?"

"No, ours is over there" he said, pointing to a patch of woods behind Murl's tent. "That one is all yours."

"I'm honored."

Her tent was a modern high-tech contraption of bright yellow synthetic fabric, fiber-glass shock-cord poles, and a ring and pin anchoring system. Conrad's was a canvas wall tent circa World War II, with ropes running everywhere and a ceiling that consisted now mainly of duct tape. It weighed a ton. By the time Margot's tent was pitched, Murl and Brash had come to greet her.

"Looks like the Martians have landed," Brash said.

"Come on, dude," said Murl. "You've seen a woman before, haven't you? At least in picture books."

"Yeah, thanks a bunch," Margot said, only pretending to take offense. "I mean, I know my hair's a mess, but I didn't know…"

"I meant the tent, smart-ass, and you know it," Brash said to Murl.

"We rarely know exactly what he means," Murl said. "So take it all with a grain of salt."

"Thanks for the warning."

Then more proper introductions were made, including handshakes, etc. then a further examination of the tent. "That is quite a contraption," Murl said somewhat admiringly. "What holds it down?"

She showed him the corner pins. "Those plus all my stuff." She threw a travel-bag and a sleeping-bag in and zipped the fly.

Brash walked around eyeing both the tent and Margot skeptically. "I think to a strong wind that baby would look more like a kite than a tent. You might want to tie it to a tree."

"Never had a problem so far," Margot said.

"Suit yourself."

"I warned you about Brash," Conrad said.

"You did."

"'Warned' you about me? What the hell's that supposed to mean?"

"Nothing bad, I assure you, but I see now why they call you 'Brash.'"

"They don't 'call' me 'Brash,'" he said. "That's my given name. It's on my birth certificate. Brash Lawrence Whitcomb III. An old family name."

"I'm *sorry*!" Margot said. "I didn't mean to offend you. Boy, I'm off to a great start. Would it be easier if I stayed in a motel? I don't want to put you out."

Murl took her hand and said, "No, it would not be a easier. We are honored to have you in our humble campsite. And if *anybody* is going to a motel, it is this rude prick."

"Screw all of you," Brash said, grabbing a beer from the cooler. "Not you, mam. I didn't mean you."

"Perhaps Margot would like a beer," Murl said.

"Thank you, I'd love one."

Though he might have hoped otherwise, Conrad had known better than to expect Brash to be on his "good" behavior around Margot. And once Brash started, it was important for Conrad to let the moment run its course, to see how Margot handled it. Would she take offense, fall apart and turn mean as Cynthia had when assaulted by the elements on the upper Cupsuptic River? The answer was immediately apparent: if anything, Margot seemed amused by Brash and by her own faux pas, and intrigued by their situation—like an anthropologist who had stumbled upon a vestigial remnant of a primitive tribe, honest-to-god trout bums, in the best sense.

Which was, in fact, exactly how she felt. So much of her time was spent guiding those who, for lack of a better term, loosely qualified as "Yuppies," even if they weren't young. It was refreshing to see the other side, but, try as she might, she couldn't think of them as "colleagues," as fellow guides or peers. They were purer than that. People like this, she'd only read about in books and magazines. To find that they actually existed somehow restored her faith in, if not guides, in fly-fishermen, and in her decision to return to her roots in the East. These men were a part of the pre-industrialized era of fly-fishing, and she liked them immediately.

Once it had been determined that Margot had already eaten and, therefore, did not require feeding, the decision was made to sit by the river in lawn chairs, to drink beer and watch the sun set. Margot had even brought her own lawn chair, made of a light-weight breathable, bright yellow fabric that matched her tent.

"Damn," Brash said. "I always wondered what it would be like to go camping with Martha Stewart."

Margot exploded with a robust laugh that sent a spray of beer towards the river. "You are too funny!" she said. "First Martians, now Martha Stewart." She nudged Conrad, sitting next to her. "You didn't tell me he was so funny."

"I never noticed before," Conrad said. He'd bet anything that Brash had not meant to be funny. He was trying to be unpleasant and rude; she just wouldn't let him. If Conrad had to pick the one moment when he fell in love with Margot, that would've been it: the beautiful laugh, the spray of beer, that said she wasn't intimidated by rude men, and she wasn't a prima donna; she was one of the boys. It had never occurred to him that *that* was what he wanted in a woman. It sounded weird, it sounded gay, but it wasn't. The fact was, a good guy was a good guy, regardless of gender. And Margot Montgomery was one hell of a good guy.

Margot, looking around and still taking it all in, said, "This all reminds me so much of Montana—the woods, the river—but you guys are a lot nicer than the guys out there."

"Didn't mean to be," Brash said.

"Those guys, the guides, wouldn't even condescend to be insulting. It was like a woman who wanted to guide did not even exist."

She had said the magic word, "Montana," and had deftly directed the attention and conversation away from herself and towards the West.

"What's it like out there?" Murl asked.

"It's beautiful." she said. "But no more beautiful than this."

Even Brash couldn't help himself. "What waters did you fish?"

She named the ones she knew they wanted to hear: the Madison, Gallatin, Yellowstone, and the Bitterroot; she even mentioned the Henry's Fork of the Snake, which wasn't in Montana; it was in Idaho, but who cared? The names carried the magic of the West, and her words cast a spell, though, in Brash's case, it couldn't last.

"So why'd you come back East?" he asked, though it sounded more like an accusation than a question.

"Partly because of the way the other guides reacted to a woman from the East. And I didn't like what was happening to the fishing either. Take the Bitterroot, for example. A few years ago that river wasn't on anybody's A list of waters. Now, there's a whole fleet of drift-boats. There are fights in the parking-lots for a place in line. Because, you know, a lot of times it's whoever gets to the fish first. So yeah, you got more fertile waters out there, more fish per mile, but that's not the whole story. Or even half of it."

"That's what we're afraid of here," Conrad said. "That's what we don't want happening. That's what Spike brings."

"But we're teaching him manners," Brash said.

"Well, you would be the one to do it," Margot said, eliciting laughter from Murl and Conrad.

"I *am* the one to do it. Somebody's got to. These pussies—pardon my French—just roll over and play dead."

"Our methods are a little more subtle," Conrad said. Then patting Margot's arm. "That's your cue. That's where you come in."

"We'll see," she said. "So anyway, as I was saying, going West gave me a new appreciation of the East. Not just attitudes towards women, but what's happening to the fishing. Take the Androscoggin. Used to be the dirtiest river in the East, maybe in the country. But now it's cleaned up, at least to some extent, and there's quite a fishery."

"Yeah, for store bought rainbows," Brash said. "Conrad told us."

"I didn't say 'store bought.' I had a nice time. Quit trying to make trouble."

"That's OK," Margot said. "He's right, they aren't native fish, but you really can't tell the holdovers from wild. They fight just as hard as rainbows in Montana. Take my word for it. I've caught them both places."

"Still 'store bought,'" Brash said. "Right off the shelf."

"Well, maybe not all of them. There're some signs of natural reproduction. People are catching smaller fish than the state has stocked."

"Hell," Conrad said, "half the fish we catch are stocked too."

"Maybe the ones you catch," Brash said. "The ones I catch are native, or if they aren't, it's not my fault. That's all I fish for—native brookies and landlocked salmon." Like an ex-smoker or born again Christian, there was no fish-purist like a former bass fisherman. Brash was now the most fervent salmonid fisherman of the three. "I strive for native fish," he said, as a statement of high, unassailable principle. "A man has got to stand for something."

"You're fortunate to still have native fish to strive for," Margot said.

They were quiet for a while, Conrad suspended in a state of blissful infatuation. Then Brash said, "I have another question. Why, in this time of national peril, when America is assaulted on all sides by her enemies, do you drive a Jap truck."

Margot laughed, and shook her head. "I think that truck was actually manufactured in Tennessee."

"Don't split hairs. It's a Jap company."

"I believe that nowadays 'Jap' is considered pejorative."

Brash made a mean face. "You think I don't know what that word means, don't you? 'Pejorative.' I know what it means."

Once again, he made her laugh, something about his silly, pouty little-boy expression struck her as hilarious. She couldn't stop laughing until, finally, Brash said, "You might not think it was so funny if you'd lost a grandfather on Wake Island, or a great uncle in the Bataan death march."

"I never heard that one before," Murl said.

"I'm sorry," Margot said, still not quite able to stop laughing. "Really, if I've offended you, I'm sorry, but, I mean, if you get upset every time you see a Toyota or a Honda or a Subaru, you must stay in a constant state of turmoil."

"You got that right," Murl said.

"I'd rather not talk about it any more," Brash said, as if the subject were just too painful for further discussion. "I'm going to bed. Good night." With that he went into his tent and crawled into his sleeping-bag.

"Have I really offended him?" Margot asked.

"I certainly hope so," said Murl.

"Well, if I did," she said playfully to Conrad, "it's your fault, because you didn't warn me about that."

"This was the first either of us ever heard of it. There's a lot we don't know about Brash."

"And some things we do know about him we wish we didn't," said Murl rather loudly.

"I heard that," Brash said, from inside the tent.

"Shut up and go to sleep," both men shouted back.

But Brash could not fall asleep immediately. He lay there listening to the river and the hushed indecipherable conversation outside the tent. He thought, all in all, he'd given a good account of himself. He never actually claimed that any of *his* relatives died in the war. He merely suggested that if any of hers had, she might have felt differently about driving a Toyota. It was a hypothetical: if A, then B. there was a big difference between a hypothetical and a lie, though naturally he didn't expect Conrad to appreciate the distinction. He was too much in the woman's thrall. Some men you couldn't protect from themselves. And some women you could not offend with words, only by denying them the limelight.

Soon Conrad came to bed and lay restlessly inside his sleeping-bag, attentive and alert. Behind the soft river-sounds, he heard movement in the adjacent tent, zippers and the soft rustle of clothing. He heard Margot's feet slide into the sleeping-bag, and he wondered what she was wearing. It reminded him of his marriage—so close and yet, so far away. The gap in his marriage was as real as the tent fabric that separated him and Margot. He felt the urge, the ache, to tear through that fabric and touch her. Brash's loud snoring, so close to Conrad's head that it drowned out all other sounds, came as a relief, and carried the promise of sleep.

6

The plan, as Margot perceived it, was somehow to utilize her feminine guile to undermine Spike Jackson's manhood, his confidence. Which raised a question in her mind: what sort of person would come up with such a plan? Presumably a woman, but not a very nice one. It was a rather bitchy plan, which raised another question: where would a *man* get the idea of using a woman as a weapon, or, worse, as a scalpel, with which to perform a pretty nasty, very personal, operation?

And finally, how on earth could a woman, even if she wanted to, threaten the manhood of someone who wore his manliness as lightly as did this Spike Jackson, who virtually handed her his masculinity on a platter? He met her wearing a *lady's* straw hat! He was waiting for her at the boat launch below the dam in this absolutely ludicrous looking, huge, floppy hat, secured beneath his chin with a little blue strap, looking as if he'd just that moment left off weeding his geraniums. "Nice hat," she said.

"The sun is waging war on my complexion," Spike said. "And the sun is winning."

He was only slightly taller than she, but muscular, with powerful forearms, fair, freckled, complexion; he was wearing waist-high Simm's waders, her favorite brand too. Excluding the hat—though it was hard to take her eyes off it—he looked every inch the prototypical guide. He had the guide's laconic speech and economy of movement.

Spike's vehicle had already been shuttled down to the takeout. Spike was ready to go once he inspected her tackle. While she was donning waders, he stripped the line from her six-weight, stretched and straightened it on the grass, then snapped off the last few feet of leader, and added a new tippet from his own supply. She might have been offended, if she hadn't been inclined to do the same herself, especially, though she hated saying it, with her female clients. Nothing worse than fishing hard for hours, finally hook a good fish and break it off on a poorly tied knot or rotten leader.

Spike tied a tiny pheasant-tail nymph a few feet behind a large stonefly nymph, and attached a fluffy orange strike-indicator about seven feet up. He left her other rod in its case and rigged his own six-weight with a sink-tip line and a big Grey Ghost streamer. "Down and dirty," he said, "at least to start off with. We'll adjust as we go."

"Should I call you 'Jonathan' or 'Spike?'" she asked mischievously as she was climbing into the boat.

He gave her a funny look. "'Jonathan?' where'd you get that."

"I don't know. Must've read it somewhere. Maybe the internet."

"Nobody calls me 'Jonathan' anymore," he said.

"'Spike,' it is then."

The dam pool was already surrounded by bank fishermen and two men casting flies from the dam itself. "Busy place," she said.

"Yeah, a little too busy. We'll go down a ways. The access road only goes a mile or so down-river. Below that there's almost no competition. Hang on."

She sat in the bow facing down-river. It was heavier water than she was accustomed to, a couple of stretches of rapids, where, even seated, she had to clutch the gunwales. He handled the boat easily, confidently. Approaching a particularly heavy section of submerged boulders and standing waves, she looked back anxiously, and Spike was smiling and seemed to be enjoying himself. She was surprised at how quickly they came to the Beach Pool, where a man—Brash or Conrad, she couldn't be sure—was casting from the shallows. Spike hugged the far shore and drifted straight through. "Not stopping here? Looks like good water," she said.

"Nothing wrong with the water, but those guys are nuts." He nodded towards the man, then noticing the new tent, added, "Looks like their numbers are growing. Just what we need, more psychopaths per river-mile."

"Are they really that bad?"

"Last week one of them threw rocks at my boat. And he wasn't even fishing! Scared the hell out of my clients. This one guy is totally unstable. You know, PTSD or something. And I'm told he has at least one firearm in camp. Not worth it for a fish, if you ask me."

"Why don't you report them to the authorities?"

"For throwing rocks? It'd be his word against mine, and what would the wardens do? They're scared of him too. None of those guys are any too stable. And they're all Registered Maine Guides, if you can believe that."

Margot shook her head, relieved that he couldn't see her smile. And to think that she had spent the night in the midst of these maniacs, and yet somehow—perhaps because she was *inside* this fortress of men, who were feared by the outside world—she'd never felt safer in her life, or slept more soundly. And from her perspective even the rude and irascible Brash Whitcomb had seemed more threatened than threatening, damaged goods.

And dear sweet Conrad had insisted on making her breakfast even though she protested that a cup of coffee and a donut, which she had brought, would suffice. "I think not," Conrad said gallantly, the margarine already sizzling and the water steaming. He fried venison and eggs, and served freshly ground "gourmet" coffee with real cream and honey, which he knew that she preferred. "Nice service in this place," she'd said.

"It's how we keep our triple A rating. You'll have to try us again sometime."

When she and Spike reached a slower section, Spike rested, stopped rowing and used the oars only as tillers to hold course or change direction.

"You know," he said, as they were drifting lazily along, "I have to say, your responses to my Client Survey Form were a bit unusual. I've only used them for a couple of years, but that's the first time any client has ever mentioned Jane Austen as their favorite writer.

Usually they'll say John Gierach or Thomas McGuane, you know, names they think a guide would recognize or want to hear. But Jane Austen, now that's a switch. Sort of refreshing."

"Are you familiar with her work?"

"Are you kidding? *Mansfield Park* is one of my favorite books. Jane Austen rocks. She rules! She kicks ass!"

"I never heard it put quite that way before." Who *was* this guy? She'd never met another guide who'd actually read Austen, at least not one who would admit it. She hadn't dared ask anyone in Montana, because they'd already branded her an "East Coast Elitist," and she did not wish to deepen that wound.

Soon Spike anchored just above and to one side of a beautiful curved deep slot, shaped like the broad blade of a scimitar, deepest near shore beneath an overhanging cedar that made access for wade fishermen exceedingly difficult. "Run those nymphs through there," he said.

She did as she was instructed. It wasn't pretty; it wasn't possible to make a pretty cast with tandem nymphs and a fluffy strike indicator. It was like lobbing a little parachute; the weight and wind resistance eliminated false casts, tight loops and all the other "poetic" aspects of fly-casting. But she managed to place the flies where she and her guide wanted. Her second time through the water, even closer to the overhanging cedar, the strike indicator dipped momentarily and then resumed its drift. "You just missed a strike," Spike said.

"It was a rock. I felt it."

"When that tip goes down, you *have* to set the hook."

"I *do* know the difference between a rock and a fish."

"Humor me, OK?" he said. "Just set the hook anyway. Even if it is a rock, so what?"

Margot gritted her teeth. So this was what the others meant by his overbearing demeanor.

The next time through the same water, the strike indicator dipped again, and this time she obediently lifted the rod, but instead of a rock, she felt the solid, live weight of a good fish. "Oh my god!" she said.

"What'd I tell you? What I'd tell you!" Spike was whooping and hollering like a kid. "Whose your daddy? Whose your daddy, now?"

But his comments were directed, not at her, but at the fish. For the next five minutes, for both of them, nothing existed but the fish, its mad dashes, its athletic leaps, three all told before it tired and came to net. It was a male salmon, nineteen inches, almost twenty, (by evening it *would* be twenty, pushing twenty one) bright and silvery, not so colorful as the rainbows on Margot's river, but, in its own understated way, more elegant and regal than her beloved rainbows, in the same way that black and white photos sometimes carry more weight than do color photos.

"What do you think of the East Outlet now?" Spike asked, as Margot rinsed her hands after releasing the fish.

She beamed. "It's everything I hoped for," she said, "and more." Her smile was as radiant as that salmon, in the context of which, all other motives for the trip had shrunk to insignificance. Gender issues, guide-on-guide grudges, girl meets boy—at that moment, nothing mattered but the river and that fish.

The minute the markets closed, Murl scurried off to the Black Toad, where Brash Whitcomb was already two beers ahead. "The rest are on me," Murl said. He'd had a good day, bought'em on the way up, caught'em on the way down. It was a gift. "Did you fish?" he asked.

"I tried the Moose below Brassua. Wall to wall people. What's the world coming to?"

"I thought you might have hung out at home, and watched for Spike."

"Conrad was making me too nervous. I hate it when he gets like that. It's pathetic."

Murl shrugged. "That's life. Everybody's got to make his own mistakes."

"Yeah, but the same one over and over again?"

"Some people are slower learners than others."

"'Slow' isn't the word for it. When it comes to women, C-Rad is retarded."

"He's a big boy," Murl said leaning back into the path of the waitress. "I'm ready for another."

"That was quick," the waitress said.

"Playing catch up."

"Speaking of…your friend here, and his friend, the other one, they've run up quite a tab over the last few weeks."

Murl whipped out his VISA card, handed it to her with a wink. She winked back. "Fishing's been good, hunh?"

"Caught a couple," Murl said.

"There's more to us than fishing," Brash said. "You shouldn't be so quick to stereotype people."

"Sorreee!" the waitress said, rolling her eyes at Murl.

"Don't mind him," Murl said.

A few minutes later Spike Jackson burst in, if anything, even more ebullient than usual. He'd replaced his silly looking straw hat with a baseball cap. He swaggered down the narrow space between tables, speaking to everyone and slapping palms of the people he actually knew, until he passed Murl and Brash, where no palms or smiles awaited. Spike gave a tight-lipped smile and slid past. "A good day, hunh?" Murl asked.

"Awesome!" Spike said, and kept moving towards his usual table of rafting guides and their girlfriends.

Murl turned back to Brash. "Now there's a broken spirit if I ever saw one."

"I'm afraid the broken spirit is back in camp," Brash said, pushing away from the table.

"I'm right behind you," Murl said.

But first he had stop at the cash register where the waitress and bartender were tallying up a thick sheaf of unpaid bills. The waitress looked up sheepishly and shrugged. "You have expensive taste in friends," she said.

"You get what you pay for."

Puttering around camp in the pre-dawn dimness with Margot reminded Conrad, for the first time in a long while, of the funny, charming little things that women did before going out in public—even for a fishing trip. Good looks was a mixed blessing for a woman: good looks drew compliments, but evidently also carried the responsibility to maintain the looks, not just a responsibility to one's spouse or lover either, but to the public at large, the same as a city was responsible for mowing the grass, planting flowers and other beautification projects for the summer tourist season.

So Conrad was hardly shocked to find Margot applying powder to her cheeks with a small brush while holding a tiny mirror. "If that's not sun block, it's a total waste of time," he said.

"Hunh?"

"You, of all people, do not need makeup."

She smiled, stowed the brush and dabbed her lips with a light patina of pink. "I'm not used to having somebody watch me do this."

"Sorry."

Then Margot tried to talk him out of making the breakfast that he'd planned for days, but Conrad would not be denied. This much he understood of the language of women: feeding equaled nurturing, and pretty much nothing ranked higher on a woman's scale of virtues than nurturing. So he insisted that she sit down and eat. "It won't kill him if you're a couple of minutes late. I promise you, he will not leave without you."

"I can't help it. I always get like this when I'm going fishing."

That part he understood, but she looked so gorgeous that he was having second thoughts about sending her off to spend the day with Spike Jackson. And his pretext for doing so seemed flimsier than ever, and he realized that what he had really wanted from the very first was this intimate moment alone, with the birds just beginning to chirp, and the river whispering sweet nothings. He'd hoped, however, for a slightly different night before.

"You know, if you don't feel like going through with this," Conrad began, "I mean, if you'd rather just hang out here, I could show you the river myself. I know it better than he does anyway. I've fished it longer."

She gave him a funny look. "But you don't have a drift-boat."

"OK." He knew better than to push it. "I just don't want you to feel obligated, that's all."

"No, I'm looking forward to it," she said, wiping her mouth, and *not* re-applying the lipstick. That could wait for later.

The next crisis for Conrad was how exactly to send her off. It was a delicate moment that had to be handled correctly. You couldn't pretend it wasn't a "moment," but you couldn't make too big a deal about it either. He wanted to blend the intimacy of a husband sending his wife off to work with the sexless innocence of parent packing a child off to school. A peck on the cheek while holding—but not hugging—her by the shoulders, and maybe, when she turned to leave, a pat on the fanny like a coach sending a star athlete into a big game. But he doubted that coaches could even pat fannies any more. The rules of the outside world were changing too rapidly; camp rules were constant, until, of course, you added a woman to the mix. Then all bets were off.

Conrad finally settled on himself as theatrical director giving last minute instructions to an actress before she took the stage. He took her by her shoulders and looked her over from a couple of angles. "You look great," he said. Then, as he walked her to the truck he added, in a confidential tone, "Remember, this guy has been giving your profession a bad name. Your job is to take him down a notch, teach him manners."

"Got it," she said.

"Break a leg." He skipped the fanny-pat.

He fixed himself a cup of coffee, sat on a boulder beside the river. He thought, all in all, he had handled it well, the morning was off to a promising start. Then Brash woke up and totally wrecked the moment.

The only thing worse than an obnoxious Brash Whitcomb was a kind and solicitous Brash. It was so transparently *phony*; at least the obnoxious version felt authentic. Conrad found this quasi-therapeutic-inquiring-into-feelings version nauseating. He finally had to tell him, "Look, I don't need a shrink. I need a stomach doctor. You're making me sick, dude. You're taking my appetite."

That produced the hurt-Brash, the man of tender feelings. He grew quiet and contrite; he even apologized for "intruding" on his buddy's "space." It was a great relief when Brash finally announced that he was off to fish the Moose River, and that, of course, Conrad was welcome to join him. "A change of scenery might do you some good."

Graciously but firmly, Conrad declined the invitation. "Too much to do around here. Another time perhaps."

"Have a nice day."

Conrad did not have a nice day; he had a terrible day. Soon after Brash departed, Spike drifted through, hugging the far shore, not slowing even for a single cast. By the time Conrad located his binoculars, Spike and Margot were out of sight, leaving Conrad to wonder, what could it mean that they passed through so quickly? After considerable thought, he decided that it was a good sign: they were moving fast because Spike wanted to get the day over with; they weren't catching fish, and he was getting his butt kicked.

Conrad considered following them down-river; he'd travel along the bank with binoculars, then he decided, no, that was too much like voyeurism, like being a Peeping Tom, and he was a bigger person than that. Besides, he'd found out the hard way that that sort of behavior could have embarrassing consequences, such as a restraining order—just because he cared enough to drive by his ex-wife's house a couple of times to see what piece-of-crap car was parked out front. Because he had been concerned, and after the split, Cynthia had taken up with some real low-life types, compared to whom Conrad was, if not a shining star, at least a diamond in the rough. She finally came to her senses, and lifted the order, but the damage to his self-esteem was done.

Next Conrad sat down with pencil and paper and tried to calculate exactly how long it would take Spike and Margot to fish the lower river, reach the dirt ramp at Indian Pond, load the boat, navigate the tote road, and then for Margot to get back to camp. If it took a boat two hours to get from the dam to the Beach Pool, how long would it take the boat to get from the beach pool to the take-out, which was maybe two and a half miles farther down-river? Assuming the flow rate was constant, and allowing for lunch. He decided to let $X =$ the flow rate of the river. No, that wasn't right. Let $X =$ the boat. That was worse; this whole exercise was bringing back even more bad memories—math class! Whoever thought algebra would have real life applications? If they'd have told him that, he might have paid more attention!

Four o'clock, that was his answer. Don't ask him where it came from. It came from the same place the answers to his math quizzes came, and *not* from the next desk either. He didn't cheat. The fact was, he kind of had a feel for math, a knack. It was just the numbers part that eluded him. The specifics could be tricky, but he was good at multiple choice. So he re-phrased the problem as follows: when would she get back? 1pm, 2pm, 3pm 4pm 5pm 6pm, or none of the above? After he factored in the length of the lower river, time out for lunch, and hooking a few fish, 4pm just sort of jumped of the page at him as the right answer.

But when 4pm finally rolled around and there was no sign of Margot, Conrad realized—silly him!—that he'd forgotten to factor in the lousy condition of the tote road and how much slower Spike was likely to drive with a woman riding shotgun.

At 5pm Conrad quit making excuses, and he opened one of the bottles of wine he'd been icing down in his cooler. A good white wine in a corked bottle. No screw cap wine for this woman.

By 6pm that bottle was more than half gone, and at about 6:30pm, when Margot, happy and unrepentant, finally bounced back into camp, that bottle was history, and Conrad was definitely feeling its effects.

"Where've you been?" he said stumbling over to her, "I was *worried*."

She gave him a funny look. "It's barely six-thirty. I didn't say when I'd be back. I didn't know."

"Right, right," he said gathering himself. "I was just afraid something might have happened."

"Poor baby," she said, patting his arm. "You shouldn't have worried." A few strands of her hair were out of place, and her shirt was damp, but she still looked good, and she smelled even better than before.

"Well," Conrad said, "Spike can be pretty careless with his boat, particularly when he's showing off."

"No, he did fine, and we caught some nice fish."

"How'd *you* do?" He didn't like the sound of "we," as if she and Spike were a team.

"Ahmm, fish-wise fine, but otherwise, well, I might have blown my lines. I mean, I called him 'Jonathan,' and did the thing with the rock, but it turned out to be a fish. A *beautiful*, big, male salmon. You should've seen it! He jumped, he ran, he did everything. It was one of the prettiest fish I've ever caught. That fish alone was worth the drive. We got a couple of others down-river, but that was the best by far. I'll never forget that fish." She stopped and thought. "I'm sorry, what was the question?"

"Doesn't matter. I get the picture."

She squeezed his arm. "I'm sorry if I let you down, but you knew it was a long shot. What could I do? Spike turned out to be a pretty decent guy. And believe it or not, bitchiness doesn't come naturally to all women." With that she gave a shrug and began collecting her gear.

"You're leaving?" he asked forlornly.

"Yep, got a business to run. But it's been great."

"I guess you've already eaten," he said, picturing her and Spike over a candlelit dinner.

"No, but I'll grab something on the way."

"I have a steak out for you. Wouldn't take but a minute."

She winced. "I'm sorry. I'll take a rain check, OK?" She was already disassembling her tent. There was nothing for him to do but help.

The collecting and packing of her possessions was somber business and brought back more sad memories, more than should have been brought back by something so simple as helping an overnight guest pack, but the collapse of that bright yellow tent into a heap of rumpled cloth seemed too much of a metaphor for his spirits. So he started talking very fast as if the sheer volume of words could re-inflate his hopes. Time was running out. Everything he'd planned to say over wine and dinner came bubbling up and pouring out: Yes, of course, he'd take a rain check; he was just glad she'd come, and sorry she had to leave so soon, but he understood. And he was sorry if his friends had been rude, maybe she would come again and they could fish together, maybe get to know each other, etc. etc. and somehow in the middle of his monologue he slipped up and called her "Cindy," and he didn't even notice or slow down. The gush of words just kept pouring out until he'd said it all, her truck was loaded, he was exhausted, and his spirits were still deflated.

Then, softly, Margot asked, "Who is Cindy?"

He flinched. "What? Why'd you bring that up?"

"You just called me 'Cindy.'"

"I did? Oh my God, I am sorry." He proceeded to apologize profusely and excessively, as if his lapse might have hurt her feelings or done her serious emotional damage, when he needn't really have worried. She was concerned, not angry.

"If you'd rather not talk about it, that's OK. I was just curious."

He wandered over and more or less collapsed into his lawn chair and stared out at the river. What a disaster. What a fool he was.

Margot perched on the arm of his chair, light as a sparrow. She tousled his hair. "What's going on here?" she asked.

"I wish I knew?"

"It's OK," she said. "We've all got baggage."

She stroked the back of his neck, and the next thing she knew his head was resting in the soft hollow between her shoulder and her neck. She pushed the hair away from his forehead, wondering how on earth she'd found her way into this refugee camp of wounded, dysfunctional men, and how would she extricate herself without adding to the damage? Her inclination was to pamper men and bind their wounds—that was how she became a guide; it was that or medical school—but she knew that some men, the better sort, wouldn't let her.

Conrad remained with one arm now around her waist, as long as pride would permit, both comforted and humiliated, and wondering, what to do next? He couldn't retreat. That was unthinkable. The only way out was to advance. So he took a deep breath and made his move. His left hand that had been resting innocently on her waist, slid down into the back pocket of her jeans bringing him one layer of clothing closer to her skin, to that achingly beautiful curvature of buttock. When she nuzzled his hair, he tipped his head up and kissed her neck and nibbled her earlobe, finally arriving at her lips, which, instead of being soft and receptive, were tightened into a huge smile. Then she kissed him quickly, sweetly, and shook her head. "Men!" she said. "You're all alike." She gently lifted his hand from her pocket and removed herself from the chair.

The way she said it, her timing, it sounded to Conrad like a huge compliment: even in his weakest moment, he wasn't so different from other men. By taking his sexual overtures seriously, instead of as the desperate measures of a drowning man, she had stopped him from drowning, and he would *never* forget it. "You're quite a woman," he said, as they were standing beside her vehicle, to which they'd walked slowly, hand in hand.

"You're not so bad yourself," she said, planting a kiss like a healing poultice on his cheek. Then she hopped into her truck and high-tailed it out of there.

7

When Brash passed Margot on the road, she smiled and waved, but did not slow down. Brash found Conrad standing at the water's edge staring off into the distance. Brash approached as delicately as if approaching a mental patient.

"How'd it go," he asked from a safe distance.

"It went OK," Conrad said, without turning around.

"You sure? Because we saw Spike at the Toad, and he seemed the same as always, maybe more so."

"Some men know how to hide their pain," Conrad said. "And who to hide it from."

"Whoa!" Brash said. "That's profound, dude. That's far out."

Conrad shook his head in amazement; sometimes Brash talked as if he were caught in a time warp. Then again, maybe they both were.

A few days later Murl received an e-mail from Margot thanking them all for their hospitality, and apologizing if she had upset their routine. There was no mention of a return trip. A few days later, a thank-you present in the form of a smoked ham arrived at Murl's apartment for all of them, with a note from Margot. "Sorry, fellows, but neither FedEx nor UPS would deliver to the 'Beach Pool on the East Outlet of the Kennebec River.' Silly them."

"A class act," Murl said, dropping the ham onto the camp table.

"As if I didn't already know," Conrad said.

"A little too classy, if you ask me," Brash said.

They didn't see Spike Jackson again until the Fourth of July, when, it seemed, everybody and his brother was on the river. The markets were closed; so Murl was in camp too, but none of them felt much like fishing. Too crowded. So they sat in their lawn chairs in the afternoon sun, drinking beer and watching the parade of bank fishermen traipse by. Every now and then, because he had the patience of a five year old and couldn't wait until dark, Brash would toss a firecracker towards the water, sometimes a whole pack. He had a battery of bottle-rockets and roman candles for later. There was an edginess to Brash's pyrotechnics; it was part boyish celebration, part war against the invaders and the infidels, meaning all intruders on that section of the river. He was feeling patriotic and even more bellicose than usual.

Murl and Conrad were relieved when, mid-afternoon, Brash moved his chair into the shade and nodded off. Soon Murl and Conrad did the same, only to be rudely awakened a short time later by Brash, shouting and scurrying about preparing a barrage of bottle-rockets. "Battle stations, boys! We're being invaded!" Then he made a high pitched, three note whistle imitating a ship's alarm.

"Would you please stop," Conrad said. "That's very annoying."

"Spike Jackson is in our territorial waters. I suppose you just want to let that go."

Conrad squinted and gazed across the river. Even without binoculars, he could easily recognize Spike's boat, and in the bow wearing his ridiculous straw hat, was Spike himself, identifiable as much by his casting as by the hat: he could throw a fly-line a mile. So who was that at the oars? Conrad shaded his eyes with his hands. The person rowing was a woman; her brown pony-tail was pushed back through the opening in her baseball cap. Then the first bottle rocket exploded above and to the right of Spike's boat.

"Stop it!" Conrad shouted.

"Twenty short, thirty right," Murl said.

"And don't you encourage him!"

"It's a holiday, dude. Just chill," Murl said, as another rocket exploded, long and to the left.

"It's Margot!" Conrad said. "It's Margot Montgomery in Spike's boat."

"All the more reason," Brash said, preparing his next missile.

Conrad ran down and kicked his bottles over. "Grow up," he said.

"Get a grip!" Brash shouted. He stood up glaring at Conrad; Conrad glared back. Murl came over and settled them down. By then Spike's boat was safely down-river, and the moment had passed. "One more shot, I could've nailed the fucker," Brash said. "We had him bracketed, dude. Just like in Nam."

"'Nam!'" Murl sputterd. "Closest you ever got to Nam was Boothbay Harbor."

"Yeah, but I read the books, I saw the movies. I know what it was like."

Meanwhile Conrad had moved away from those two, was gazing wistfully into the distance. Brash and Murl exchanged knowing looks. "It's now or never," Brash said.

"Go for it," said Murl.

Brash nodded, took a deep breath, and gathered himself. "Intervention time!" he said. "Time to rock-and-roll, lock-and-load."

Brash rearranged the lawn chairs into rough triangle, facing each other, feet nearly touching. Then he beckoned Conrad over. "Sit down, my friend. We need to have a little chat."

Being addressed as "my friend" led Conrad to expect the worst. "*Now* what are you doing?"

"For once, will you just listen?"

"Humor him," Murl said, handing Conrad a beer. "It'll be easier for all of us."

Conrad took his beer and reclined in his chair. Brash and Murl sat upright. Brash fidgeted, struggling for words. "Look, here's the thing," he finally said. "It's this Margot deal, but it's more than that. It's the whole woman thing. You got some issues, dude."

"No shit," Conrad said. "What a shock that is."

"*Awright*, then," said Brash. Maybe this would be easier than he thought.

"You gotta accept the fact that it's not happening with you and Margot, you know? You gotta let it go."

"OK."

"That's it? 'OK?'"

"What do you want from me?"

"I want some feeling. I want some anger. It's part of the grieving process. It'll help you let go."

"But I'm not angry at her. Anything but." He couldn't explain the gratitude he felt. Sadness too, but mostly he was grateful to her.

"You're not? You don't mind being Spike's pimp?"

Conrad shook his head in dismay. "You have such a disgusting way of looking at things. You really do."

"You just gonna roll over and play dead?"

"If I was her, I'd have probably preferred Spike too," Conrad said.

"I can't believe you said that," Brash said, turning to Murl. "It's worse than I thought. She's crushed his manhood, destroyed his ego."

Conrad laughed. "She hasn't destroyed anything. Can't you get it through your thick head? She's not a destroyer."

"A battleship maybe?" Murl said, trying to add a note of levity.

Conrad held his head in his hands. It was hopeless to attempt to explain the gratitude he felt, the love even, for Margot. If anything she'd *restored* his sense of manhood, such as it was, and, more importantly, his sense of womanhood. Margot had reminded him of what being with the right sort of woman was actually like, when he'd been in danger of forgetting, or, far worse, falsely remembering.

Brash was at a loss for words. Exasperated, he turned to Murl, who had nothing else to offer, his last jest having elicited a scowl from Conrad. Finally Brash threw up his hands and said, "I just don't get it, dude. I don't understand you. I will never understand you."

Conrad looked his good friend in the eye and said. "I'll never understand you either."

"No?"

Conrad shook his head. "But that's OK. In my opinion, understanding other people is vastly overrated."

"It is?"

He nodded. "In my opinion, it is. Acceptance, that's what counts. Just accepting people, particularly your friends, mystery and all."

Brash rocked back in his chair. "Whoa, dude! You did it again." He sat forward, excited. "No, really, that is deep, man! Where do you get this shit?"

"I don't know," Conrad said. "From her, I guess." He didn't say which her, because he wasn't sure himself.

Brash sat dumfounded, shaking his head, then holding his head in his hands, lest it fly away or explode. Then he turned first to Conrad, then to Murl and with a bewildered look asked, "*Now* what do we do?" That made them both laugh.

When they stopped laughing Murl said, "I say we go fishing."

"Now *there* is great idea," Conrad said. "That's the best idea I've heard all day."

Brash didn't like it. "Go fishing? It's ninety frigging degrees, in case you haven't noticed. There's a million A-holes on the river!"

"All the better," said Murl.

"Exactly," said Conrad. Then to Brash, "We go expecting nothing. Imagine how satisfying it could be to catch a fish under these conditions, the sense of accomplishment."

"Not to mention," Murl added, "how much fun it would be to haul out a couple of nice fish right under some flat-lander's nose."

"Well, I guess if you put it like that..." Brash said. Fishing as conflict, as battle, kicking butt—now, that he could relate to.

In that way the three men survived a potentially treacherous afternoon with their friendship more or less intact, and no new legal charges added to the list. That alone put the day in the win column; they even caught a couple of fish. Then the holiday passed and summer was upon them, real summer, the doldrums, when the sun bore down and the fish held deep. For Brash and Conrad fishing season was over, and guiding season had arrived.

Anybody could catch fish in June. July and August were the months that separated the amateurs from the pros, the Master guides from the nouveaus. June guiding was nothing more than showing people where to fish. Too much of that and you'd put yourself out of business; you'd cut your own throat. That's why Conrad and Brash did not offer June guiding. Or September. What they offered was more than a chance to catch a couple of fish; they offered the Total Maine Fly Fishing Experience.

The typical day started at the Beach Pool, set up like a classroom, complete with folding chairs they'd rescued from the local transfer station. They could accommodate up to eight students at a time. With a two month season, you had to pack them in. The morning session consisted of basic introduction to tackle, knot-tying, and casting technique. Conrad did the talking; Brash handled the demonstrations. Then it was the students' turn. Then time for lunch, the Gourmet Shore Lunch, including white wine, which, in the heat of the day, often left the students and their guides lethargic and ready for a siesta. Not a problem; tents and cots provided gratis. No other guide service offered that!

After lunch came "Essentials of Fly-tying," with emphasis on caddis-flies in preparation for the highly anticipated "evening hatch," the hope being that, before the day was done, students would catch fish on flies that they had tied themselves!

About 4pm they'd begin the trek to the "secret pool," where, more often than not, there'd be rising fish. True, most of the fish were chub, fallfish, not a highly desirable species in some elitist circles, but there would often be a few brook trout mixed in, and in the fading light of day, it wasn't always possible to be one hundred percent sure what species rose to take the fly. If the client didn't get a good look and wanted to believe it was a brook trout—"That was a brookie, wasn't it?"—the least the guide could do was be supportive—"Sure looked like one to me." And if the fish escaped or broke off—fairly common on two pound tippet—that cinched it. It was "almost certainly" a brook trout, and a "good one" at that. And the sports were regularly reminded that hooking the fish was the big thing, having the fish take the well presented fly, which, just a few hours earlier, the client had tied himself. Quite an achievement.

If a fallfish were brought to hand, and its identity undeniable, the client would often express disappointment—"damn chub"—whereupon the guide's job would be to educate and correct the client's error: "chub" was a slur, like "Jew" or "Jap." The proper name was "fallfish." "*Semotilus corporalis*," Conrad would pronounce majestically, as he held a specimen for all to see and admire, before resuscitating and releasing it as gently as if it were a trophy brook trout. "It takes at least as much skill to hook old Mr. *Semotilus* here as it does to hook a brookie. Sometimes more." Then Conrad would give a little historical sketch on the derivation of the name "fallfish," at least one man's theory, his: "Fallfish were part of the autumn harvest for pilgrims and Indians. The fall larder. *Semotilus* is a native fish," he'd add. "Unlike smallmouth bass, largemouth bass, rainbow and brown trout, *Semotilus* is an authentic part of Maine's heritage, her history. Some like to claim that cod was the fish that made America great, and maybe for the coast, that is correct. But in these inland waters we like to think it was *Semotilus*." That "we" was intended to include Conrad Larue among the curators of Maine's precious history. Then he'd wipe his hands, pat his angler proudly on the back, "Well done. You've come a long way in one day. A very long way." The thing was—what made it work—he meant it all. Fish species, let alone size and number, was irrelevant to the true essence of fly-fishing. How many angels could sit on the head of a pin? Or for that matter, the point of a hook? The principle of fish, any fish, rising to a fly, real or otherwise, at the shimmering interface of worlds—there was your miracle; the rest was window-dressing.

They hadn't seen Spike Jackson for days. They thought he might have been guiding smallmouth bass trips on Indian Pond, or maybe he took some time off. Then one hot August evening after a desultory day astream, as Brash and Conrad were re-hydrating themselves at the Black Toad, Spike wandered in. He looked different, more subdued. He wasn't in fishing gear; just jeans and a T shirt, and he didn't gab, greet and glad-hand on the way over to his usual table. He just nodded and smiled. And when he sat down with his rafting buddies and their girlfriends, he didn't swing the chair around cowboy-style and straddle it backwards. He sat regularly, a little stiffly, and when a beer was brought, he merely sipped it, and then swirled his mug absentmindedly in the rings of condensation on the table top. Soon he rose, shook hands with the men, hugged the women—he was saying good-by! Then, with a deep breath, he turned and approached Brash and Conrad's table. "May I join you for a minute?" he asked diffidently.

"Free country," Brash said, but Conrad was in a more charitable mood and offered him a chair.

"If you don't mind, I'd like to buy you guys a beer."

Brash just shrugged—a free beer was a free beer—but Conrad said, "Sure, that would be nice. What's the occasion?"

"I'm coming to that," Spike said, as if he'd been rehearsing and didn't want to lose his train of thought.

They sat quietly, a little awkwardly, until the order was taken, then Spike said, "Look, I know we haven't always seen eye to eye on things. And I probably stepped on a few toes along the way. But I want you to know that I respect what you guys do, and have done, and what you represent. And if I crowded you, I'm sorry about that. But what I wanted to tell you is, I'm not going to be in your way anymore. I'm relocating. The East Outlet is all yours. Enjoy." He lifted his glass.

"You're what?" Conrad asked.

"I'm heading west. Well, western Maine. And eastern New Hampshire. I met someone, a woman." And then, clearly oblivious as to how the meeting had actually come about, Spike proceeded to describe Margot Montgomery, her fishing, guiding and business skills, her personal charm—he wished they could meet her. Who knew? Maybe one day they would have the chance. He and Margot were going into business together. Spike was going to work out of her shop on the Androscoggin River. She would guide the New Hampshire side. He would guide in Maine. No other shop covered both states. "It's a great niche. A unique opportunity," he said, excited about the business prospects.

"So, with this woman, it's mainly a professional relationship?" Conrad asked.

Spike smiled sheepishly and said, "Well, there's a little more to it than that. It's too early to say how much more. Time will tell."

There was another awkward silence, not broken until Conrad extended his hand and said, "Well, good luck."

"Yeah, all the best," Brash said but he didn't shake hands.

"Thanks. And I wish you guys well too. I mean it." With that, he rose from his seat, made a final, wistful little wave back to the other table and walked quickly from the bar.

Conrad and Brash just sat there. Brash was afraid to speak or even look at his friend, until Conrad said, "Guess he wasn't such a bad guy after all."

"Jeesum!" said Brash. "One beer and suddenly he's a great guy. I mean, everybody's got a price, but *one* beer!"

But for Conrad it was either upgrade his opinion of Spike or downgrade Margot, and it was too late for that. In Conrad's mind, that moment with her had been preserved and was as sepia-stained as a precious old photo. That happened plenty of times with fish—his head was cluttered with fish pictures—but it was unprecedented with a woman. Yes, his mind had probably air brushed the rough edges and exaggerated her beauty, and over the years his mind would probably continue to embellish, same as with a fish. But so what? It didn't matter any more what the literal "truth" was; it was a trophy memory, a treasure. The challenge down the road would *not* be to avoid bitterness, but to keep the lady's memory from diminishing future women. If his mind applied the same principles to women as it did to fish—and why shouldn't it?—he would be OK, because he had some really great trout and salmon stashed away in his brain, and they never once interfered with the pleasure of his next fish. For that, and for other things, he was very grateful.

Murl strode in a few minutes later, and it was obvious from the look on his face that he'd met Spike outside and that Murl *knew*. He sat down and patted Conrad on the back. "Well, congratulations. Looks like your plan worked."

"Like a charm," Conrad said, lifting his glass.

"Yeah, right" said Brash sarcastically.

"Hey, we wanted to get rid of Spike. We got rid of Spike. Not to mention, my friend, that you still owe me one hundred dollars."

"You don't have to put on a brave face for me, dude," Brash said. "You give me the word, I'll go kick his ass."

Conrad shook his head in dismay. "That's your solution to everything, isn't it?"

"You might be surprised just how often it works," Brash said indignantly.

"I would be surprised."

Brash turned to Murl. "The jerk buys him one beer, and now they're all buddy-buddy."

"Everybody's got their price," Murl said.

The foursome at the other table, the two rafting guides and their girlfriends, looked a bit bewildered now that Spike was gone. Finally, since Spike had blazed the trail, one of the guides got up and came over to the three fishermen. "Hey, would you guys mind if we joined you?" the guide asked. "I mean, we're always looking back and forth at each other, and, what the hell?"

"Personally I could use a little intelligent conversation," Conrad said.

The guide looked pained. "Damn, I don't know about that. But the girls can probably help."

So the two couples came over and squeezed in around the small table. A cute blonde with multiple piercings sat next to Conrad. In the cartilage of her ear, like rivets, was an arc of cubic zirconium, fake sapphires and rubies. The table was so crowded that her ear almost touched Conrad's face, and when he turned towards her, the stones were so close that he couldn't focus, and the many facets of the fake jewels caught and bent the light into a dazzling array of reds, blues and silver. "That is *so* beautiful," he cooed, his lips so close that he had only to whisper the words that she alone could hear. She laughed so hard that the others wanted in on the joke, but she said, "Nope. Sorry it's our secret." She patted Conrad's leg.

Conrad glowed, but Brash Whitcomb looked away, weary, yes, but ready at a moment's notice to come to his best friend's rescue.

The River Dwight

Whenever someone asks me how I got started in the indoor fishing business, I say it was luck. I don't say if it was good or bad luck. I let them decide.

I'm a Registered Maine Guide by profession, which is quite an honor, but, as my wife Marie liked to remind me, it's not a paying profession unless you actually take people hunting and fishing. Well, I don't hunt; so right away, I was at a disadvantage. And I fish under very strict guidelines, flies only and no kill; so my clientele was on the small side. Which suited me fine; I was more into research and development anyway. Marie said that what I did wasn't "research;" it was "reading." She had other words for it too, most of which you won't find in your thesaurus. Marie's a Licensed Practical Nurse, and she was getting more practical every day.

The fact was, I'd come up with some pretty good ideas over the years. I held patents to Dwight's Titanium Rod Tips (they'll bend, but they *will not break*) and Dwight's Threaded Ferrules (no more seized rod-tips; no more separations in mid-cast). With so many four-piece travel rods coming onto the market, I saw threaded ferrules as a growth industry, though so far the manufacturers had missed the boat. I encouraged Marie to try and look at these patents as annuities. "One day they'll pay off. You'll see." She said, "May be, but in the meantime, I'm sticking to Tri-State Megabucks. Better odds." Marie had lost a lot of faith in me over the years. Maybe we both had.

I did most of my research in the Maine State Library, and it was there I came up with the idea of indoor fishing. But I didn't get it out of books. That day I was tired of reading. My eyes were weary, and I needed a break. I walked over to the window and watched the snow fall. Barely December and already we were into our third storm. As I watched the yellow stains and dog mess disappear, I thought, "Wouldn't it be nice if our lives were like that, if all our mistakes and false starts could be covered over with something white and pure, that in the spring would wash away, carrying our miscues with it."

Soon I grew tired of watching snow and thinking big thoughts, so I wandered back through the museum section of the library, 12,000 years of Maine history. The first 11,800 was a tale told in stone. The stones were said to be implements, tools. Each minor modification of rock was supposed to represent some great societal advance, in some cases a whole new culture. To a person with even a speck of imagination, it was a very depressing exhibit. Heck, my threaded ferrules represented a bigger advance in fishing implements than these people had made in ten thousand years. Not meaning any disrespect to Native Americans, but I believe if I had lived in those days, I could have cut, conservatively speaking, centuries off their development.

Next there was a section on Pilgrims and colonial life, which everyone who lives in New England was supposed to love, but which bores me more than the rocks, because most of these items—trivets, quilts, and other quaint knick-knacks—were still available in catalogues. I say, let it go. Let it die!

Then came the logging and lobstering exhibits, followed by a series of Maine Wildlife Scenes—stuffed animals in their natural habitat, meaning plastic trees and papier-mâché rocks. At least there was a logic, a consistency of concept that ran unbroken through the beaver-bog scene, the salt-marsh scene, the moose scene, deer scene, and bear scene, but then the concept was shattered by the trout stream scene, because here was movement: water flowing over actual rocks into a small pool, at the bottom of which, finning quietly, looking expectantly upstream, were real live fish! Brook trout, char, if you will, whose sleek lively shapes heaped shame on the other, inanimate, exhibits.

This was new; this was stunning. I leaned against the glass and stared longingly at the fish. I wanted to break through the pane and lie down beside the flowing water. I don't know how long I stood like that, before I felt a light, bird-like tapping on my back. It startled me; I wheeled around and saw a small, harmless-looking, gray-haired lady.

"I'm sorry," she said. "I didn't mean to startle you, but it's closing time. You wouldn't want to get locked in, would you, and have to spend the night?"

"Oh, could I? Please!"

She sized me up. "You poor man," she said. "No place to stay?"

It was an understandable mistake—the long black hair, the beard, the heavy boots, worn jeans, flannel shirt, the lanky haggard look, and the mental institute just across the river. "Well..." I said.

"I could call a cab. They could take you to a shelter."

"Thank you, but that's not necessary. But tell me this, who designed this exhibit?" Now that the mood had been shattered, technical questions of hydrology, oxygenation and finance replaced my longing. The woman looked puzzled. "I'm still trying to make something of my life," I said with absolute sincerity. "I haven't given up yet."

"Good for *you*." She jotted some information on a chit of paper. "Call this number in the morning. Ask for Mr. Eliot. Tell him that Bernice Bilodeau said to call."

"Thank you," I said. "Thank you very much."

She reached into her wallet.

I said, "No, really, you don't have to..."

"Don't be silly," she said, stuffing a twenty-dollar bill into my shirt pocket.

"God bless you," I said. "You will not regret this. I promise."

Outside, the snow looked like the stuff of angels, and, though I wouldn't have wanted to know the Ph, it tasted sweet as powdered sugar. This was indeed a charmed moment: my first backer, my very first investor. I made a mental note: a lifetime pass for Bernice Bilodeau to the River Dwight. And on my way home I bought a six-pack of Molson and a bouquet of flowers.

There was a time when Marie would have been touched by the gesture. On those occasions when I forgot that those days were over, she was quick to remind me.

"I don't even want to know where you got the money," she said.

"Like I always said, 'Follow your heart, and the money will find you.'"

"God, Dwight, you're not twenty years old any more, or even thirty. Or even thirty-five, for that matter."

"If you don't like the flowers, have a beer. Have two beers. They might improve your disposition."

I popped my second Molson, warmed myself by the woodstove and thought how really well-preserved and fetching Marie looked in her uniform, how pleasingly the pure white offset her black hair and pale blue eyes, how the cut of her dress suited her narrow waist and wide hips. I was feeling pretty good. "Yep," I said, "you had better mark this day down in your little book, because on this day, your husband has had a grand idea."

"My little book is full of your grand ideas. There's not room for any more."

"No, no, your book is full of bright, little ideas, brainstorms, but this, my dear, is different. I have expanded my vision."

"Well, don't, OK?"

"Too late. You can't put the genie back in the bottle."

"Then God help us." She tossed the flowers into the firebox and opened and beer. "I have prayed this day would never come. I mean literally prayed, and regularly ever since you spent that whole year working on that dumb mayfly pattern. Day after day, night after night, tying and re-tying, filling the sink and tub with trash, not sleeping, walking the roads for dead animals, stinking up the house with skins. I said the same prayer every night. I said, 'God, please don't let anything run him over and keep his thinking small,' because I could see then that, if you ever came up with a big idea, it would kill you, kill us both."

I'd never heard any of that before. "That hurts," I said. "That really hurts. That you don't have any more faith in me than that."

"I'm sorry, Dwight. I am truly sorry, but I am not going to lie to you."

"Bernice Bilodeau has faith in me. She believes in me, but own wife…"

"I suppose that's the poor soul you fleeced for beer money."

"You know what you are? You're a traitor."

"I am. I know it. My faith in you should be inexhaustible, but it isn't, and now you know. And now I'm going to bed. I've been on my feet all day, and I am very tired and I'm going to bed."

"One day you won't have to be on your feet all day."

"No, I'll be in a wheelchair."

For the record, Dwight's Perfect Mayfly was featured in *Fly-Tyer's News*, Vol.VII, Issue #3, complete with color plates and tying instructions. True, the commercial prospects haven't panned out so far, but who is to say that, even as we sit here, that fly's reputation is not spreading by word of mouth, or that soon L.L. Bean and Orvis will be forced to carry it and pay me royalties? Who really is to say?

At this point I would like to thank the Taiwanese for having wrested the shoe industry from these labor-beleaguered shores. Not only have they put affordable footwear within easy reach of all Americans, but they also left in their wake a windfall of old, abandoned buildings available to young, or even middle-aged, entrepreneurs at most reasonable prices. I believe this more than compensates for what they have done to us in Little League.

Also I would like to thank Mr. Ronald Reagan for deregulating the Savings & Loan industry, thereby liberating thousands of loan officers from the tedium of home mortgages. All over America, even in Maine, loan officers were ready to celebrate their freedom, and what better place to start than with a local project that would simultaneously revitalize downtown Augusta, give people a warm place to congregate on cold winter nights, keep teenagers off the street, and, "Who knows? It might curtail the use of drugs and reduce the rate of adolescent pregnancy," I said to the loan officer, one Theresa Bilodeau, no relation to Bernice, but a handsome woman in her own right, a rugged business-like blonde, who wore her hair in a tidy bun and was outfitted in a conservative gray suit. But so was I!

Plus I had shaved my beard, trimmed my hair, shined my shoes and borrowed a briefcase. I had also rehearsed my presentation in front of a mirror, there having been no other interested parties available. And my presentation was a doozy, if I do say so myself. I could tell Theresa was impressed as she flipped through the computer printouts, plans and blueprints.

"This is all very interesting," she said. I thanked her. "And this project may do everything you say it will, but keep in mind, Kennebec National is not a charitable organization. And the first question we have to ask ourselves is, is this project financially viable? Because if the answer to that question is no, then your project is not going to do any of these other things, is it?"

"Of course, not, but I think you'll find the answer to that question on page four." I had made some earnings projections based on the number of fishermen we could accommodate, charges per hour, food sales, entry fee, and so on. "You'll have to admit, those are pretty impressive numbers."

"Indeed they are," she said, after looking them over, and there're some pretty bold assumptions underlying them. Such as, that you will be operating at full capacity."

"Cut those figures by twenty percent, and we still turn a profit."

"Assuming your expenses are in line. Which raises another point. Your previous business experience, or lack thereof. We do like to see previous experience."

"Why? So you can weed out originality, so you can keep repeating yourself?"

"No, actually it is so that we can remain solvent."

"Theresa, tell me this, how much business experience did Colonel Sanders have?"

"I haven't the faintest idea."

"Not a lick, but he made great chicken, and the business took care of itself."

"Is this going to be a franchise?"

"Might be. You don't know. You might be looking at the Colonel Sanders of indoor fishing." I leaned across her desk and looked her right in the eye. "Theresa, don't let this rinky-dink town cramp your vision. Don't let it make you afraid to think big. I've seen it happen."

"Didn't happen to you, did it?"

"No, and I don't intend to let it."

She closed my folder. "Well, this is fascinating to say the least, but the first thing I have to do is run these building estimates by my consultants. Then I'll need to confer with the powers that be. This will take some time. Not too long, ten to fourteen days. I'll be in touch." She stood to shake my hand.

"Ten to fourteen days?" I asked.

"Is that a problem for you?"

"No, no problem whatsoever. Nice talking to you."

Fourteen days of hell, of suspended animation. I didn't dare leave the house, or clean it or change my clothes. I held myself in a state of readiness. This was the turning point of my life. My past and future would pivot on this moment, I was sure. And I believe that I can be forgiven for a momentary lapse of judgement, when, on day fifteen at 0900 hours, the loan came through, and I wrapped the check in Marie's dinner napkin. When she found it, she wept, but they were not tears of joy.

Probably I don't need to say this, but it's not easy living with a non-fisherman. Non-fishermen tend to view fishing and everything connected with it as a form of goofing off. I have dedicated my life to disabusing people of that notion. Judged by this criterion, my life to that point had not been a resounding success. Possibly I took out my frustration on my workmen.

I drove them hard. I exhorted them with a bullhorn. I put a stopwatch on their lunch hours. I also helped pour concrete, move boulders and plant shrubs. After ten weeks of work, I felt as if I were earning their respect, but, of course, it wasn't *their* respect that I was after.

I kept Marie away from the project until we had at least a rudimentary river, though not yet one that would support life. That would require gravel, oxygen and an even temperature, but as soon as we had running water, I took Marie for a visit. I wanted her to see the river, to hear it, feel it, and believe in it, and in me.

I made her keep her eyes closed until we were standing on the balcony like the king and queen of England looking down upon our loyal subjects, who, fortunately, were far enough away that we couldn't see their facial expressions. The men all stopped work and looked up at us. They had my permission, my blessing, to take a break with pay. Naturally there were a couple wolf whistles directed at Marie.

"They like you," I said.

She glared at me and took a step back. "They're looking up my dress."

"Look over there," I said. "See that stretch of river? We're going to put spawning gravel in there. One day fish will actually reproduce in this river. My river. Our river."

"Pardon me, but I don't see any river. I just see a lot of dirt and concrete."

"Right," I said. The river bed was dry. I gave the thumbs up to one of the men; he flipped a lever, and a great gush of water poured forth, inundating the serpentine river bed, creating riffles, pools, and deep mysterious runs.

"OK," Marie said. "I've seen it. Can I go now?"

"That's it? That's all you have to say?"

"Dwight," she said. "Dear, sweet Dwight, I never for one moment doubted you were capable of creating such a thing as this. Only that you could sustain it. Twenty years ago, I found your flashes of brilliance and moments of glory charming. But don't you see? Flashes and moments just don't cut it any more. Consistency, stability, that's what I find sexy now." She looked me in the eyes—such sadness. "I'm sorry. I guess I got old on you. Or middle-aged. Please forgive me." She kissed me on the cheek and hurried out of the building. Her tears ran down the side of my face.

The workmen were looking up at me; they were unnaturally quiet. I lifted my bullhorn. "She likes it," I said, "but she's disappointed that you aren't farther along. Now back to work."

Marie elected not to attend our grand opening. It was probably just as well, since it didn't turn out quite the way I planned. Apparently people had misunderstood our advertisements. They thought the place was a theme park, and that the river was a waterslide. Some showed up with inner tubes. Others wanted to rent towels. I had to make an announcement over the PA system. "This is not a carnival ride," I said. "This is a place to fish. There'll be no swimming, no tubing, no canoeing in this river."

That led to an ugly scene, children crying, women shouting. When that group cleared out, a mere handful of fishermen were left, and they wanted to buy worms. "We don't sell worms," I said. "It's fly-fishing only, catch-and-release."

And where were all the fly-fishermen? I'd made a slight miscalculation and opened in June, the peak of fishing season.

Meanwhile the river itself performed magnificently. It produced a steady hatch of mayflies throughout the morning, the only indoor mayfly hatch in America, perhaps in the world. By folding it like ribbon candy, I had fit nearly two hundred yards of river into my building. The different stretches were separated by low hills and a blend of real and artificial vegetation. Trails linked the better pools. Beside the prime waters, I'd placed picnic tables. But I had left several good sections unmarked with poorly maintained trails. These would be the rewards for the adventurous fishermen, same as in real life.

A family of swallows had found my place and nested in the rafters. Opening day they swooped and dove above the river, feeding on hatching mayflies. "I'm glad you appreciate this place," I said. "I wish more people did." I consoled myself with the knowledge that many great artists were not appreciated in their lifetimes.

In August when Maine rivers over-heat, trout head for spring holes where they hang out until fall. Fish-hogs find these spring holes and slaughter untold numbers of trout. Ethical fishermen seek alternatives: largemouth bass, yard work or quality time with the family. Now there was a new alternative in town, and right on schedule, fly-fishermen—the entire local chapter of Trout Fishers United—arrived at The River Dwight. Unfortunately they did not come to fish, or to praise me, but to protest the blackfly experiments that were being performed in my river.

If I neglected to mention these experiments, it was out of modesty, not shame, for I was proud to have biologists on my premises. I saw their presence as another example of the River Dwight serving the community. Also these biologists were my sole source of mayfly larvae. They provided mayflies; I let them use the river for testing *Bti*, a bacterium used to control blackflies, a pestilence in Maine, also, of course, and importantly, a food source for growing trout, which was what concerned Trout Fishers United. No other waters were available for study, because *Bti* was banned in Maine, never mind that it was used in other New England states.

On the day of the visit I was adding and rearranging stream bed debris on a deep intriguing bend. Mayflies were popping up all over. I had heard the group was coming, though I didn't know why. I had set the water temperature at sixty-five degrees, which triggered the mayfly hatch. "If you want our patronage and support," the officious chapter president said, "these illegal, immoral experiments will have to stop."

I climbed out of the river and looked him over. He was average height, lean, narrow face, and wore wire rimmed glasses, new jeans and tassel loafers. I said, "Do you realize that *Bti* is used routinely in many other states?"

"That doesn't make it right or mean it's safe."

"Are you a biologist?"

"No, I'm a lawyer."

"A lawyer? And you presume to instruct me in morality?"

"Right," he said. "The old 'kick-the-lawyer' routine. Let me just tell you one thing. If this situation isn't corrected, not only will you not get our business, but we'll be going public with our information. We worked damn hard to keep *Bti* off Maine rivers, and we will not have our work undone by you."

"Well, I worked damned hard to get *Bti in* my river. I believe in the scientific method, and I assure you that the River Dwight will not be blackmailed by frustrated politicians posing as fishermen."

As the group turned to leave, there was a heavy splash behind them, where a large trout rose for an escaping mayfly. A dozen heads turned back towards the water; necks craned, and several members exchanged furtive glances. I knew that eventually they would be back. No real fisherman lets politics stand between him and a mayfly hatch for long. I just wasn't sure I'd still be in business when they returned.

This was an unexpected setback—betrayed by my target demographic!—and a difficult one to explain to my creditors. So I decided that for the time being that the best recourse was to ignore them. Easier said than done. An insistent lot, these creditors and generally unsympathetic to the entrepreneurial spirit. Never mind that this spirit is what made America great. I found creditors, on the whole, to be rather rude. They sent threatening notices through the U.S. Mail. They left discourteous messages on my answering machine. Even Theresa Bilodeau, in whom I placed the utmost faith, was getting feisty.

Then Marie moved out. Quite in keeping with her personality, there were no theatrics to her departure, no melodrama whatsoever, just the quiet orderly assembling of her possessions and the latching of suitcases. I had never noticed before how well a suitcase latch could mimic the hammer of a gun. Really quite a startling imitation.

Marie paused at the door. "I don't want to fight about money," she said. "I just want what's rightfully mine."

I said, "Fair enough. According to my calculations, you now owe Kennebec National eight hundred and fifty thousand dollars."

"Cute."

"I walked over to the door. "I'll turn this around, yet. You'll see. One day we'll look back on this little episode and laugh. This is going to be good for me, Marie. It's going to inspire me to work harder and be more creative. This could be just the incentive I need. Thank you for having the wisdom to do what needed to be done."

"Don't mention it. Would you mind watering the plants until I get situated?"

"That's the least I can do."

Different people handle stress in different ways. Some drink, some smoke, some take drugs. I fish. After Marie moved out, I set up housekeeping beside the River Dwight. I moved into a pup tent beside a beautiful run I had dubbed "Marie's Run." It was an exact replica of the museum pool, considerably enlarged.

I've heard it said that "No man is an island." Well, a man is not a river either, but he's more like a river than an island, and he can learn more from a river. For instance, even oceans contain rivers. There's a lesson in that: rivers don't just drain land. Rivers are more than water responding to the call of gravity. They're living entities. They link continents; they connect us all if we let them. And when we forget those connections or deny them or try to sever them, the fish are there to remind us.

For example, one night I caught a twenty-inch brown trout. No big deal? Consider this: I did not stock the place with browns. I stocked it with brook trout, because they're easy to catch. Browns are too finicky, and this one was no exception. He rose steadily at the head of the deepest pool on the river but would not take a dry fly. At first I thought that my fish were getting selective. "Don't tell me that," I said. Selectivity, though an admirable quality in a wild fish, could kill my business. Then I realized the fish was nymphing, and that was why he wouldn't take a dry.

He took a small Pheasant Tail nymph on the first cast; I set the hook with a sigh of relief. The fish jumped and I realized, it wasn't a brookie; it was a big brown. "What the devil!" I said. "Where did you come from?" He had to come from the Kennebec, because that was where I got my water and where my effluent went, but there were screens, pumps, and filters. A unit must have failed, but I would worry about that later.

The fish fought hard, but I had a heavy, 3X tippet; I tightened the drag, shortened his runs and soon wore him out. I dragged him onto a patch of gravel and grabbed him with both hands. As he lay gasping for air, his mustard yellow sides speckled brightly in red and black, the businessman in me said, "Kill him." Browns that size are cannibals; he would eat his weight in brook trout every week. I took out my pocket knife and prepared to rap him on the head, but the fisherman in me stayed my hand. Truth was, I was honored by this fish's presence in my river, however it was he'd gained entry. My river had received the approval, the blessing, of a wild fish, and that far outweighed the criticism of my skeptics and creditors.

Instead of killing him, I gave him a kiss, then waded into the river and revived the fish in the current. I held him longer than was necessary, somehow not wanting to say good-by. Finally the fish lost patience and freed himself.

Meanwhile Theresa Bilodeau was having a relationship with my answering machine. They were not getting along. No matter how conciliatory she sounded—"We want to work with you, Dwight"—or how subtly threatening—"We're bankers not realtors"—or not so subtly—"Don't force our hand"—she got the same recorded message.

The only message I deigned to answer was Marie's. "Where're my plants?" she asked. "I want them back. You had no right to take them."

To which I said, to her answering machine, "Your plants have found a new home. They are very happy here, but they do miss their mother. Please feel free to visit. We are open seven days from six to ten, three dollars an hour for adults, twelve and under are a dollar-fifty. Thank you for calling the River Dwight."

Name, rank, and serial number, that was my philosophy. If they wanted more, they knew where to find me.

Funny how much genuine peace and solitude a man can find beside an artificial river. In some ways it was better than the real thing, because there were no chain saws buzzing in the background, no drunks on ATV's, no radios. Just the sound of the river at whatever flow-rate I wanted, in whatever season. If only I could have shut out the other world forever.

But I couldn't. There were bills and letters and nasty messages. Soon I had the same beleaguered feeling I sometimes had in the real Maine woods, when I'd sense the outside world slowly closing in, the spray planes, logging trucks and chainsaws. Gradually I came to realize that I couldn't escape the so-called "civilized" world.

Whether in the form of financial pressures or treachery of the paper industry, one way or the other, civilization was going to have its way with what was left of wilderness. The best I could hope for was that in the wake of the chainsaws and ATV's some new form of wildness would arise, like grass sprouting in sidewalk cracks, or, for that matter, wild brown trout breaking and entering a man-made river.

Be all that as it may, there's still only so much crap a man is obligated to take, and I was getting sick and tired of the steady stream of letters the TFU folk were sending to the *Kennebec Journal*. So I fired off a little salvo of my own, in the form of a full page add:

> *While the River Dwight wholeheartedly supports Trout Fishers United and its goals of protecting and enriching cold water fisheries, we sincerely regret that this support is not reciprocal. We further regret that TFU allows itself to be represented in the press by a small-minded, mean-spirited, loud-mouthed minority of its members. We abhor its unfair characterization of our facility and of the legitimate scientific research being conducted on our premises.*
>
> *We would like to reassure our loyal patrons that the River Dwight is in no way "polluted," and that Bacillus thuringiensis israelsis (Bti) is a totally innocuous organism, and perfectly harmless to humans. We would remind our patrons that yogurt is made from bacteria and wine from yeast, though this is in no way intended to imply that Bti is fit for human consumption or is of nutritional or medicinal value.*
>
> *Finally we would like to assure our faithful creditors that this is a minor, temporary setback that will in no way affect our long-range profitability. Third quarter projections remain as robust as ever. These things happen; then they pass, but the River Dwight will abide forever.*

The very next evening on my way up the street to buy a paper to see how the TFU boys handled that, who should I run into but Theresa Bilodeau?

"Theresa," I said, "what a surprise. Long time no see. How've you been?" I tried to get around her, but she reached out and grabbed my arm. "You can't run away from this, Dwight," she said. "This is not the type of relationship you can simply turn your back on when the going gets tough."

"Damn!" I said. "You've been talking to Marie."

"She came to us. She was concerned. She still cares, though I'm not sure exactly why."

"She cares about her plants."

"She cares about a lot more than that. Now stop acting like a child and come inside."

I looked at my watch.

"Not later," she said. "Not tomorrow. Now!"

"Ok, ok, great. I want to talk to you. We have a lot to talk about, but give me five minutes to fix the place up. It's a mess. Five minutes, is that too much to ask?"

"Is there another exit?"

"Theresa!"

"Five minutes," she said. "The meter's running."

One thing I was particularly proud of, in addition to the mayflies, was the computerized rheostats that controlled lights, sound, air and water temperatures, wind, and, with the magic of track lighting, the exact solar arc of every season—except winter. There was no winter on the River Dwight.

With more time I believe that I could have come up with a more suitable program for Theresa. If only I had known her better, her tastes in music, her moods and emotional needs. But I didn't have more time; so I went with my old favorites: a mid-June morning, assorted finches and phoebes, and Tammy Wynette's "Stand By Your Man." Marie and I both liked it; it was our song. With Theresa it was shot in the dark, but what did I have to lose?

I ushered Theresa inside into total blackness. "I can't see a thing," she said. "And it's cold." She shivered, and I placed an arm around her. "It is pre-dawn," I whispered. "Imagine that we have just driven two hours to the trailhead. Listen to the river. Hear it?

Now look to the east." There was a faint orange glow on the far wall. A bird chirped, and a soft warming breeze whooshed through the foliage. More birds. The orange intensified; the center filled with red, and the chorus of "Stand By Your Man" synchronized itself to dawn. When there was sufficient light, I took Theresa's arm and escorted her down the narrow trails towards the river. We stood at the water's edge and watched morning emerge in all its artificial glory. A trout rose in midstream.

"Did you see that?"

She nodded.

Then the music subsided, and the moment passed, and it was morning like any other summer morning. "So, now what do you think of the River Dwight?" I asked.

She shook her head in what I took to be amazement. "I think I know why you've been late with your payments."

"You didn't like it?"

"I didn't say that."

"It was the music, wasn't it? It was a cliché. If only I'd had more time to prepare. I can do Billy Joel, Thelonious Monk, James Taylor. You name it."

"I believe you. Completely. I think that's part of the problem."

"What? It's overdone?"

She looked at me and smiled and nodded. It was a sweet, sad, eerily familiar smile. "You shouldn't have come to the bank for a loan. You should have applied to the Maine Arts Commission."

It was Marie's smile, and I was about to hear what a clever fellow I was, and I was sick of it, even if I'd brought it on myself. "I'm not an artist," I said. "I'm a businessman."

"You could've fooled me."

"I fooled a lot of people, but the fact is, I never had an original idea in my life. Everything I've ever done has been begged, borrowed or stolen. Including the idea for this river."

It felt good to admit that. I felt like a weight had been lifted from my shoulders and a veil from my eyes. I could see clearly what had to happen next. The river told me: trout were making redds; they were preparing to spawn in this very run, and those trout and this river had to be protected at all cost. I didn't have the right to let them be destroyed. The fact was, the dream had outgrown the dreamer, and the purity of my original vision seemed trivial compared to the living reality of the river and its fish.

I turned back to Theresa, who was still eyeing me with sympathy and concern. "Theresa, I said I was a businessman. I didn't say I was a *good* businessman."

She nodded and seemed relieved by my confession, as if now my rehabilitation could begin.

I said, "It's possible that I might have overestimated the amount of income fishermen were going to generate."

"That sounds plausible."

"By the same token, though, I may have underestimated other potential sources of revenue that I'm just now beginning to explore. The truth is, Theresa, I have expanded my vision of the River Dwight. Walk over here with me, would you?"

We cut through a wooded section to my campsite. There was the tent and my Coleman stove and my fly-rod propped against a tree. "Here's a little concept I've been working on—camp sites beside the river. Theresa, think of all the people who get camping gear for Christmas and have to wait five or six months to use it. How many of those people do you think would like a chance to try out that new sleeping-bag or that new tent in the winter? Beside a river, a river with real live fish in it?"

"Interesting concept."

"I could easily expand my fly-fishing shop to handle camping gear. It would be a natural tie-in. I've pretty much decided to add a few other stores, maybe on the second floor, not to obstruct the skylight, but, you know…"

"A mezzanine?"

"Exactly. You read my mind. And maybe a little boutique." Marie always wanted a boutique.

"Sort of a mall concept."

I winced. "Well, I wouldn't call it that," I said, "but *you* can if you like. But it couldn't interfere with the river. That's the one rule: everything revolves around the river."

"Of course, it does. It wouldn't work any other way."

"You do understand, Theresa, that these renovations are going to require some additional funds. Probably we should talk about restructuring the loan."

"Probably we should," she said.

I could see that word meant a lot to her. "Restructuring." It sounded responsible and business-like. So I used it several more times, and I kept talking like that until the last vestiges of pity were gone from her eyes.

Whitcomb's Raid

Like all men of conscience, Brash Whitcomb practiced catch-and-release. The difference was, he didn't always put fish back where he found them. Phone book, dustpan, or smallmouth bass—in his hands, things had a way of getting misplaced.

The night of his arrest he'd already released a half dozen smallmouths into Desert Pond, barely a mile from Torsey Pond where he'd taken them, on flies, of course. He wouldn't fish any other way, even for bass. Not many fly-fishermen in central Maine even bothered with bass. "Rough fish," they called them, like perch or pickerel, as opposed to "game fish" like trout and salmon, supposedly the only fish worthy of flies. But Brash was from "away," Virginia to be exact, and he knew good fish when he found them, and bass of both species were fine game fish. "Rough" fish? Damn right they were; that's what made them "game."

Once, a trout fisherman had bragged to Brash, "Whenever I catch a bass out of that pond, I throw him up in the bushes. One less bass is how I see it." Which made Brash want to throw up his lunch in the bushes, but a man had to watch his mouth around Mainers, especially on the subject of rough fish. And once Brash had decided to take action, the less said the better.

The Maine fisheries people took the same benighted attitude; they had no choice. Politics, not biology, forced their hand. They practiced what Brash called "salmono-culture." But single species fishery was no healthier than single species forestry. They were both unnatural, and had to be enforced with poisons, and, in the case of fish, with armed wardens, some of whom, though they meant well, tended to be deficient in "people skills."

They apprehended Brash on a dead-calm June night, a perfect night to fish, warm and sultry, with the water still cool, and the smallmouths in the shallows. The soft evening air had a milky haze to it that reminded Brash of the South, and it made the sun, which was setting behind a stand of pines, resemble a fuzzy pumpkin sitting on a picket fence. The surface of the pond bulged with possibility, like a volcano about to erupt, as if the surface tension could barely contain the pressure building from below. Which was pretty much the case. The first brown drake rose near Brash's canoe, struggled to shed, then spread and stretched its wings, floated momentarily like a tiny schooner, then lifted off and flew away unscathed. The next was not so lucky.

That first bug was like a fuse igniting the lake—not a feeding frenzy, but a slow, controlled explosion of insects and fish. Brash cast to a deep, promising swirl and waited. The fish rose again a few feet to the right of his fly. He covered that rise, and the bass rose another few feet farther right. Now Brash had the fish's pattern; he cast fifteen feet to the right of the last rise. He twitched the fly once, and was about to twitch again when the fish nonchalantly sipped the fly, and Brash nonchalantly lifted the rod tip, and that ended the nonchalance. The fish dove, and when that didn't work, he tried to fly, did one flip then another. Every time he took to the air, Brash dropped the rod tip—he "bowed" to bass same as he would to salmon—which left the fish pulling against nothing. Until the line tightened again. It had to be dispiriting for the bass to feel so free one moment—no resistance to his head shaking leap—and the next moment to realize that he was still tethered. "Don't despair," Brash said. "It's only temporary."

Soon he lipped the fish, a nice one, close to three pounds. He strung it through his lower lip; stringers were illegal in Maine, as well they should have been, but why should a felon worry about misdemeanors? Six counts of "Felony Transplantation of Fish" were the charges, one for each fish, and two counts for "Attempted Transplantation," for the two left on the stringer.

Eight fish were more than he usually caught even during a mayfly hatch, but when Brash was moving fish, he moved as many as he could. He believed—and research supported him—that a school of fish was a family unit, and Brash believed in family values, even if his own attempts at family hadn't exactly panned out.

He paddled quietly back by the faint light of the stars, the blade of his paddle dipping into the black water like a quill into a well of ink. Beside the canoe, his bass swam like obedient, leashed dogs, not bucking or pulling, but evenly, as if they came willingly. Or so he liked believing.

His beat-up old Chevy waited in a narrow, barely noticeable pullout within twenty feet of the water. He kept an aerated tank in the trunk. It was a simple set-up; all the parts came from a local pet store. The oxygenator was battery powered; so it wasn't suitable for long distance trips, but Brash worked close to home. ("Think global; act local," was his motto) He shoved the canoe as far up onto the marshy shore as possible and lifted the whole stringer with one hand and opened the trunk with the other. He flipped on the aerator, dropped the fish, stringer and all, into the tank and quietly closed the trunk. He would come back for the canoe. Without the canoe on top, there was no way to associate his vehicle with the act of fishing.

A tote road paralleled the stream that connected Torsey and Desert Ponds. He drove as far up it as he dared, out of sight of the main road, shut down lights, engine, aerator, lifted the stringer, heavy with writhing, vigorous fish, and ran through the dark, tripping more than once, until he reached the shallow, weedy, shore of Desert Pond. Shallow and weedy meant bass habitat not trout. As his eyes adjusted to the dark, his fingers worked the stringer snaps, and the fish slid one by one to freedom. None required resuscitation—the sign of a well managed operation. He was down to the last two fish, when the blindingly bright light came on behind him. And the shouts. "On the ground! On the ground now!"

"The ground is wet," Brash said. "Can't I at least get on dry land!" He turned towards the light just enough to see silhouettes of two men, crouched and holding guns out in front of them with both hands, like in the movies. "I'm unarmed," Brash said. "For crying out loud!"

"Well, we're not unarmed. So lie down. *Now*!" One warden had a high pitched, frantic voice; the other man's voice was hoarse, like he was accustomed to shouting.

Brash lay down. He had one leg in the water, soaking wet. The rest of him was in the mud. One warden ran over and grabbed the stringer, which Brash had been holding in his right hand, not sure what to do. The warden lifted it into the air triumphantly for his partner to see. "Two smallmouths," he said.

"Son of a bitch."

"At least put them back into Torsey," Brash said. "There's no need to kill them."

The one holding the stringer shook his head. "No can do. They're evidence now. They come with us. And so do you."

The other warden came over and placed a knee in Brash's back, cuffed his hands, and said—in the hoarse voice—that Brash had the right to remain silent. "In fact, I'd consider it an obligation," he added, ratcheting the cuffs a little tighter, and digging his knee into Brash's back as he rose from the ground. "Oww. That hurt. Do they really need to be that tight?"

Without saying a word, the man lifted Brash by his shirt collar and shoved him roughly ahead of him down the tote road. Every time Brash stumbled on a rock or root, the warden steadied him and held him up with the cuffs. "You're going to dislocate my shoulder," Brash said. "I've already got a bad shoulder. You dislocate it, then you'll really be sorry."

Brash weighed only about a hundred and fifty pounds, but he'd seen his share of fisticuffs, to which his pushed-in nose attested. But he'd pushed in few noses in return, but that was in his youth.

"Don't hurt him, Brad," the one in back said. Then, so his buddy wouldn't think he was getting soft, he added, "The son of a bitch! You know how much trouble the state went to reclaim that pond?"

"'Reclaim?' That's a good one," Brash said. They rotenoned naturally reproducing populations of bass and replaced them with hatchery trout. "More like genocide, if you ask me." Maybe you had to have been raised in the South, surrounded by monuments to a lost cause, to see the destruction of fish in such grandiose terms, but, be that as it may, Brash took it personally.

"But nobody asked you, did they?"

"I told you, you have a right to remain silent."

"Yeah, well I got a right to talk too, don't I? This is still America, isn't it? We still got free speech?" In his youth, he didn't think of Maine as even being part of America, much less the North. Maine was north of North, like a foreign country, and "Maine Yankee" was much different from a regular Yankee. A Maine Yankee, as he understood it, was not a town-burning carpet-bagger, but a hard-bitten old lobsterman who lived close to the land and the sea, like a lot of Southerners. It wasn't until after he actually moved to Maine that he learned that Mainers had been heroes, to their way of thinking, at Gettysburg and took pride in the fact. But by the time Brash learned that, it was too late; he'd fallen in love with Maine, its rocky soil and streambeds, its deep cool ponds. He had discovered fly-fishing.

Brash was relieved when they finally reached the pickup, which had a tiny back seat into which, with an unnecessarily hard shove, they deposited Brash.

As the wardens eased their vehicle out onto the road, they talked as if he wasn't even there. "I bet he's the son of a bitch who did Umbagog."

"Wouldn't surprise me. Maybe Moosehead and Indian Pond too."

"That's bull," Brash said. "Those are native brook trout waters. I'd never do that." He had nothing against trout. He loved trout, just not to the exclusion of other species of fish. That would be discrimination, which he opposed with every fiber of his being. In fact, it was that opposition—almost heroic at times—that accounted for the curvature of his nose. He was no redneck, he was no racist; if he so loved the South, he would've *stayed* there.

The night was so dark, that when Brash tried to look out the window, all he saw was a mug shot of his own craggy face and bent nose looking back at him. Add tattoos, knock out a couple of teeth, he could have been looking at a police documentary, starring him! Funny thing was, even though he looked like a criminal, even though technically he *was* one, he didn't *feel* like a criminal.

Brash was quiet for a while, but it was a thirty-minute ride to Augusta, and he had a lot on his mind. "Look," he said, with a more conciliatory tone, "I know you fellows take your work seriously, and I respect that. And you have the law on your side. But, you have to know, history is against you." Neither man said a word; so Brash continued. "You can't hold back the forces of nature. Desert Pond is much better suited to bass than trout. You know that as well as I do. All I'm really guilty of is being ahead of my time."

"We got plenty of bass waters in the state already," the driver said. "We don't need any more."

"Who are we to say that? Why not let the fish decide? Why not let the fish live wherever they chose?"

"Where they chose or where jerks like you chose?"

"The ones you killed with rotenone, I didn't put those in there. They got there on their own. Why couldn't you just leave them alone? Don't fish have rights?"

The driver snorted, as if Brash had said something funny, but he was serious. It might have sounded crazy, it might have even *been* crazy, but he considered moving those fish an act of civil disobedience, akin to Rosa Parks' refusing to surrender her seat on the bus, though obviously less important. But a man could only fight the battles that found him, and Brash fought for fish.

And just because he disapproved of the South's doomed cause didn't mean he couldn't admire its heroes or adopt their tactics. Brash's hero and role model was Colonel John Mosby, another Virginian, who, with a small but daring band of raiders, operated fearlessly behind enemy lines, sort of like Brash. And, Brash had a dream that one day the state of Maine would wake up and recognize his own contributions to black bass, and *maybe* they'd add his name, Brash L. Whitcomb III, to the list of Maine fly-fishing legends, such as Carrie Stevens and Fly-Rod Crosby. Crazier things had happened. For example, Colonel Mosby studied law while he was in *prison*, for a shooting a fellow student, then won a pardon and became, of all things, a lawyer and war hero. Compared to that, Brash's ambition seemed modest and his so-called "crime," trifling indeed.

After a long silence, the driver asked, "You're not from around here, are you?"

"I am so. I live right here in Mt. Vernon."

"But you're not *from* here?"

Brash sighed; he could see where this was heading. "I've lived in Maine for fifteen years."

"And before that?"

"Virginia."

"I thought so," the other one said knowingly.

Brash shook his head. He knew that the real reason they hated bass was not that they were "rough" fish, but that bass were from "away;" they weren't native Mainers. Therefore, they were unwelcome. Elsewhere people praised diversity; taught it in schools and preached it in churches. Then after church and after school, the same well intentioned people went out and poisoned bass. Go figure.

"Let me ask you something," Brash said. "How do you guys feel about the Somalis moving to Lewiston?"

"What does *that* have to do with anything?" the driver asked.

"It has everything to do with it." He wasn't accusing them of racism. Maine's population was, or had been until recently, too homogeneous to foster racism. He was accusing them of something worse: color-blind xenophobia—hatred of anything and anybody from "away." Brash knew not only what it meant but how it felt to be on the receiving end of that—all because he had a southern accent.

"Point is," the driver said, "you broke the law. And we caught you doing it. End of story."

"Save the rest of that crap for the judge," the other one added.

Next day the authorities confiscated Brash's car and all its contents, same as if they'd busted a drug dealer or, in the old days down South, a bootlegger. The vehicle, his "fish car," was no great loss. He had another, newer, one for personal use, but he had money in that fly-rod, and the aerator tank wasn't cheap either. Before they released him, they set up a meeting with a court appointed attorney.

The man looked more like a Maine Guide or a "good 'ole boy" than a lawyer—barrel-chested, burley, and wearing corduroy trousers held up with red suspenders. He wore a green chamois shirt and sported a full beard. He had a gruff way about him that made Brash wonder. "Are you really a lawyer?" he asked. "Or some kind of 'paralegal?'" The attorney laughed; naturally Brash liked him right away. And the attorney seemed amused by Brash's attitude and his willingness to suffer for it. He said it was a "refreshing" change from his usual cases, drugs and such.

He had already reviewed the particulars of the case and come up with a "game plan." As long as Brash didn't screw it up by contesting the charges. "I'm pretty fed up with guilty people pleading innocent," the lawyer said. "Just because they get a free attorney."

"Well, I guess in some ways I am guilty…" said Brash.

"That's a step in the right direction."

"…but I was sort of looking forward to my day in court."

"Well don't, OK?"

"No?"

He shook his head. "They would throw the book at you. They'd make an example of you. See, there're a lot of people pretty unhappy about rough fish being put where they don't belong. Last week somebody caught a smallmouth bass in the Rapid River!"

"I had nothing to do with any of that."

"Maybe you did, and maybe you didn't. It doesn't matter. See, being from away, you don't understand what a brook trout means to these people. It's more than a fish. It's a symbol of a way of life, a threatened way of life. You go putting bass in trout waters, *any* trout waters, hell, you might as well burn the flag."

"But that's not what I did. I put bass in *bass* water."

He shook his head. "You don't know your Maine history. Way back when, Desert Pond held trout, *wild* brookies, and there're people who, if they don't remember it, they remember their father or grandfather talking about catching a 'mess of brookies' for breakfast out of that very pond, the one you desecrated."

"Damn."

"You didn't know that, did you?"

"But they have to let go of that. They can't live in the past forever." He'd seen firsthand what damage that could do.

The lawyer lifted his index finger. "They'll let go of it when they're good and ready, not when some out-of-stater tells them to."

The attorney's plan was to go to the judge and suggest that they teach this flatlander a lesson, that they really rub his nose in it, and not with a jail sentence. Something worse: community service, 1500 hours in the state fish hatchery, feeding and caring for little brook trout. Then the perpetrator would see for himself how much hard work went into raising trout, how many dedicated people's livelihoods depended on hatcheries, and so on and so forth.

"I don't much like fish hatcheries," Brash said.

"All the better."

"...unless, you know, they're releasing fish into a place where they'll survive and reproduce. But just to put a fish in the water so some worm-dunker can catch'em and eat'em? What's the point of that? Why not have the hatcheries do home deliveries like they used to do with milk. Save everybody a lot of time and trouble."

"You'd prefer jail?"

"Those are my choices?"

"Well, there's a small mountain of evidence against you, not to mention what amounted to a full confession in the truck, *after* you'd been read your rights. If I may say so, my man, you are not cut out for a life of crime."

"Civil disobedience was how I saw it."

"That either."

And that is how Brash Whitcomb came to occupy his current position as all-around handyman at the Briar Hill Fish Hatchery. He mowed the lawn, he cleaned the raceways, he fed the fish—tossed handfuls of food pellets to ravenous trout, kind of fun, his own little feeding frenzy. He liked it there, but he had *not* gained a new appreciation of trout, because he *already* appreciated them. Brash was never anti-trout in the first place. He was pro-trout, pro-salmon, pro-bass, pro-perch, and pro-pike. He was pro-fish in *all* their many wonderful forms and manifestations.

The hatchery employees were nice too; they didn't hate Brash for what he did. They saw it as "tomfoolery," of which they were capable themselves. For instance, a few years back, a couple of the regular employees got drunked up and caught (and kept and ate!) some brood stock on hook and line. "Right out of the pens! Four and five pound brookies," his informant said. Which they might have gotten away with if they hadn't bragged to their buddies and—talk about not cut out for crime—taken pictures! Word got around. Witnesses talked. "Those two boys copped a plea and they are gone," the man said. "Had the same lawyer you did, if I'm not mistaken," he added, then roared with laughter.

When he finished laughing, Brash asked, "What'd they catch them on?"

The informant gave him a funny look. "Beg Pardon?"

"Nothing. Just making a little joke."

The man wandered off.

Joke hell, when Brash looked back, he didn't see a raceway; he saw running water filled with trout, surrounded by a low fence, very low, without a single strand of concertina wire on top. It was still summer, and the evening sun, filtered through the overhanging oaks, cast a lovely glow upon the flowing water. If he squinted his eyes just so, the nearest raceway bore a very strong resemblance to his favorite set of riffles on Spenser Stream, which used to hold some very nice trout, but hadn't for years. Even in its heyday, it had never held trout like this.

Hatchery workers kept state hours, meaning out by five. That left a lot of daylight. It would be nothing to get back in. No hatch to match either, but he knew what these fish wanted: a pellet fly, a single clump of dark green chenille on # 16 barbless hook. Barbless because, of course, he would immediately release his catch.

Michaud's Fine Rods & Flies

The first fall after we met, I moved into Jack's dilapidated farm house outside Augusta, Maine. While Jack tied flies and built rods, I fixed up the place, a small gray Cape connected to a barn that didn't have a right angle in it. That's my profession, interior design. No office, no overhead, just a business card—"Anna's Interiors"—a mailbox and an answering machine. I deal in concepts. You could say I'm an artist, and my canvas is other people's homes. Nice concept, huh? Then winter came.

There's a brutality to Maine winters that isn't conveyed by calendar art. It's not all ice formations on lobster boats. It's air so dry you have to add water before it's fit to breathe. Days shorten and the world shrinks: the inside of your house, your car, your place of work, the inside of your head.

By mid-January I was feeling lost at sea with no land in sight—spring and fall beyond the horizons of my memory and imagination. One sub-zero evening, I was particularly restless. Deep cold does that. It's intimidating. Trees and timbers pop; pipes seize; pressure builds in people same as in the plumbing.

Jack was tying flies, as usual. I could hardly remember how he looked standing in the river with the wind in his hair and a fly-rod in his hand, which is how he looked when we met, on the upper Kennebec. He was guiding my father and me for landlocked salmon. His waders were cut like overalls and, with his straw-colored hair swirling around his head, he looked like a big farm-boy. Now he looked about as romantic as an accountant. He didn't smell the same either.

"We *could* go to Florida," I said, apropos of nothing, except that every winter my dentist-father fished the Florida Keys.

Jack didn't even look up. "And spend more money in one week than I make in a month of guiding?"

"I didn't mean just for a week," I said, speaking slowly as if my thoughts were just that moment forming. "I meant for the whole winter."

I went over and knelt on the floor beside him. "What I mean is, you could guide down there. In the Keys. People do it all the time. I've read about it in magazines. These guides work in Alaska or Montana in the summer and fall, then in winter go somewhere warm. Jack, I've seen this type of fishing. You'd love it. It's nothing to learn. Just tides and about two new flies. With your talent, you'd learn it in a week."

"I've got enough around here to keep me busy."

"What? Tying flies and building rods? You can do that down there. Heck, with the money you'd make guiding, you wouldn't need to tie flies."

"Not just that. Patrick and I have some things going on the river." He and Patrick were trying to re-open the Kennebec to migratory fish, a commendable goal—in the Spring!

"The river! Jack, wake up! There is no river now, just a block of ice. You can write your angry letters from Florida."

Jack put down his fly-tying tools and looked at me. "Anna, you should have figured out by now that I'm not a migratory-type person. I'm a Mainer. This is where I belong. If you want to take big, expensive trips, you should hook up with a dentist, somebody like that. With money."

"Jack, darling, I don't want to be rich. I just want to be warm."

"Oh, why didn't you say so?" He reached over with his foot and opened the damper to the wood stove. The fire that had been smoldering roared.

"That's really funny," I said. "You bastard." I screwed the damper shut and started pacing the room—four paces. I could almost reach up and touch the ceiling. "You know who you're starting to remind me of? My mother. Really. Not my father, my mother."

"She seemed nice enough to me."

"Right. You know what else I think? I think you're afraid to go to Florida. I think you're afraid you couldn't make it down there with the big boys. You'd rather stay up here and be a big fish in a little pond, pound that one piece of water over and over again, day after day."

"I can find fish anywhere," Jack said matter-of-factly. "Anywhere there's water."

I plopped down onto the old, worn sofa and looked up at the ceiling. The problem was, to have a violent scene, you needed violent people, and Jack, for all his crude habits, had the heart of a poet. I talk big, but when push comes to shove, I tend to plop onto sofas and stare at ceilings.

The first year my father fished the Keys, he returned tanned, refreshed, full of fish stories, and full of himself. I had never seen him so invigorated, so handsome as when he burst through the door. "I have seen the future," he announced, "and it works. But it doesn't over-work."

I laughed and hugged him. That sort of comment was so un-like him.

My mother, a native Mainer and non-fisherman, was not impressed. "No bettah than a summer person," she said.

"I never once said I was," he replied.

It was such a sensible answer that I wanted to applaud and shout, "Bravo, brave father," but I knew better. So I did the next best thing. I took up fishing.

I bought magazines and catalogues and checked books out of the library—the classics, such as Bergman, Brooks, Haig-Brown, and the modern masters too, such as Kreh, Whitlock, Sosin and Apte. I became fluent in the language of fishing; I learned the names of the flies and their histories. I knew the tensile strength and modulus of all commercially available graphite, though naturally in fresh water I preferred Tonkin cane. I learned my knots also: Turle, Bimini Twist, improved clinch, blood, nail, and Duncan loop. If it was in print, I could tie it.

One night my father "caught" me practicing my Bimini Twist on the back of his rocking chair. He stood silently and spellbound, as I spun my magic, deftly twisting, wrapping, hitching and re-hitching. This was no harder for me than Cat's Cradle or Jacob's Ladder. And, of course, this wasn't really practice. Practice had been earlier in private. This was my audition.

When I was done, he sat down into the chair with his *Wall Street Journal* and said, "If you really want to go that badly, next year you may."

I almost wept. The poor man, the poor son-less man, so alone and outnumbered in that house.

Jack's friend Patrick reminded me of a rabbi—dark clothes, dark hair, dark beard, intense gray eyes—but he was actually an artist, fishing guide and fly-tier. He painted and sculpted fish. Not scenes of people fishing, not trees and mountains and rivers. That would have compromised his principles. He painted fish, period. And I'll say this: he could make a fish look as fierce as a Bengal tiger or as graceful and majestic as an eagle. Because that was how he saw them, how he believed them to be. Jack said Patrick was the best painter of fish in America, maybe the world. Maybe so, but he was the worst friend Jack could have had. They were too much alike, even had the same religion. It shared a symbol with Christianity, but they didn't worship Christ. They worshipped the symbol, the fish. They were heathens, nuts, and their conversations worried me.

No matter where they started, they ended up on fish, then the river, then the Augusta dam, which they were determined to eliminate. They would talk of congressmen and coalitions, but as the evening wore on, the talk would inevitably turn to dynamite. Dynamite was direct and didn't require the complicity of politicians. And once the dam was breached, once people saw the river flowing freely through their city, they would not allow it to be rebuilt. Then the upriver dams would fall like dominoes. So what if Jack and Patrick got caught? It would be worth it.

"Not to me it wouldn't," I said. "I'd rather have you free than an open river. What good is an open river to a lonely woman?"

They looked at me like I was a heretic. "I'm sorry," I said. "I just don't want you to lose sight of what's at stake here. The human perspective, I mean."

They thanked me for my input and resumed their conversation. Detonators, that was the night's topic. Sometimes a woman has to take matters into her own hands. Men like Jack and Patrick, they need taking care of.

If there's been one rap on me as a woman, it hasn't been my looks (cute face, perky features, short black hair, firm body) or my brains (I run my own business!); it's been that I manipulate. So what? It's human nature to manipulate. (Look what we've done to the environment) Not only that, it's my profession. Really, doing a life is not that different from doing a large living room. The same principles apply: first you get to know your subject inside and out, his wants, needs, desires, dreams and doomed visions. From those fragments, a theme emerges. In Jack's case, the theme was, naturally, fishing. Fine, I could work with that. I would need help, however, Patrick's help, and he would need mine, though naturally he didn't know it at the time.

One day I phoned him. "Patrick, I've been thinking about you a lot lately, about your work, your career. Jack says you're the best painter of fish in America, maybe in the world."

"Because I told him that."

"Let's say it's true. The question is, why aren't you rich and famous? Why aren't your paintings hanging in the finest homes in Maine, in America?"

"Well, for one thing, I don't have enough to go around."

I hate it when he gets laconic. "*Exposure*, Patrick. For an artist, exposure is the name of the game. You have *got* to get your work before the public."

"I'm listening."

"Suppose it could be arranged that your works—and *only* your works—could be displayed in a proper setting. Not just a setting, a context: a fly-fishing shop and art gallery all in one. I'm thinking elegance: fine art, fine merchandise.

"What do you want from me? Other than the work?"

"Fifteen percent on the sales of your work, a free sign, and maybe some weekend coverage."

"A sign?"

"It'll give you something to do with your evenings. If you'll pardon me for saying so, Patrick, you boys need a better project than blowing up dams."

Have I mentioned that I once re-did my father's office? Formica and vinyl make a statement, I told him, and it's not the sort of thing I'd like said about me. I went with dark hardwood, what I call my "Merrill Lynch" look. He almost died when he got the bill, but he paid up, and—here's the point—he never looked back. "Best investment I ever made," he said. A lovely man.

For Jack's sign, hardwood was out. It's difficult to carve, and it weighs a ton. We went with stained basswood instead. The top half was a huge brook trout in bas relief, carved in meticulous detail, painted in full spawning colors. Below the trout, in block letters: Michaud's Fine Rods & Flies.

Late one evening Patrick helped me lug it in and lean it against the sofa. Then, giggling and whispering, we snuck into the kitchen and shared a beer. I tried to talk him into staying until morning, so that we could share the moment of Jack's discovery, but he said, no way. We were both a little scared.

After Patrick left, I couldn't sleep; so I just sat up and waited until sunrise. I'd forgotten how far south of us the sun rose in winter; it struck Maine a glancing blow at best. Sort of made you feel neglected. When Jack came staggering out in his skivvies, half awake, he almost tripped over the sign. "What the hell is this?" he asked.

"Looks to me like the sign fairy has been here," I said.

He went into the bathroom, then came back out. "Seriously, Anna, what have you done?"

"Read the card."

In a tasteless moment in the wee hours, I had taped a red bow to the top of the trout's head like a little cap, thereby inadvertently violating a cardinal rule: never get cute with fish. Jack tore off the bow, tossed it into the trash and read the card.

"My birthday's not for weeks."

"Then call it a late Christmas present, OK? Let's not split hairs." I grabbed him from behind and held him tightly, and told him everything. "I know it's pushy of me, but I've found the perfect place, in Hallowell, on Water Street—can you believe that?—right beside the river, *your* river, Jack."

"I just can't believe that Patrick was in on it. The son of a bitch."

"He's not a son of a bitch. He's your friend, and your partner. If you let him be."

Jack unlocked my arms and kneeled down for a better look at the sign, which was as wide as his arm span. I went outside for a walk. When I left, Jack had his eyes shut and was examining the trout with his fingers like a blind man.

There were beaks of ice along the road, marking a sort of miniature glacial retreat. I broke the fragile edges with my boots. Around here spring is always a difficult delivery; we have to do what we can to help. When I got back, Jack was still kneeling half naked before his sign.

I had leased an interesting space—long, deep, and narrow, not unlike an aquarium. I scattered Patrick's fish throughout, hung them at different heights along the walls, dangled carved pieces from the ceiling. I even suspended a carved brown trout beneath a skylight, looking up, as if through its own watery window—a very aquatic concept, if I do say so myself.

Fly-tying materials were arranged according to colors on a free-standing, motorized rack, which rotated just fast enough to make the furs and feathers undulate, as if alive in a light current. When the sun hit that display, it lit up like a piece of living coral. The rods were racked, assembled and strung, along one wall. Want to try one? No problem. I'd run an elevated walkway across the back parking lot to a casting platform at the river's edge. You could actually test your rod over fish. How many shops offer that?

When it was done, even Jack was impressed. "I had no idea you had so much talent," he said.

"You think anyone who can't cast a hundred-feet is retarded."

"That's not true, but this…this is really something." He walked timidly around like a visitor.

"Don't be afraid to touch," I said. "After all, it is your shop."

"Must be," he said. "The sign has my name on it."

"You'll get used to it. Now shut your eyes." I escorted him past a partition to the unfinished rear of the shop: concrete floor with a single small rug, wood stove, stack of wood, straight-back chair with a plain work bench for tying flies and building rods.

He opened his eyes and I handed him an "EMPLOYEES ONLY" sign. "This is your space," I said. "No customers allowed, not even girlfriends if you don't want them."

Tears welled up in his eyes. He turned away, then turned back and embraced me.

Soon spring arrived and summoned Jack back to his beloved river, that section of the Kennebec that flowed from Moosehead's East Outlet to Indian Pond—several miles of rapids, riffles, slots and chutes, and deep pools and many landlocked salmon, Jack's favorite fish. Except for that word "landlocked." His goal in life was to unlock them, to liberate those fish and that river.

Jack's summer camp was a wall-tent on a wooded bluff over a deep run known locally as Colorado Canyon. When the morning sun struck the boulders at its bottom, the stones glowed like gold nuggets. We had a fire-pit and crude, wooden bench where, protected from biting insects by the swirling wood smoke, Jack and I would spend our weekend evenings listening to the river. Later we would fall asleep with the aroma of that smoke still in our hair and the sound of the river in our ears.

We both rose early; Jack was off to meet his sports, and I was off to the river. On weekends there was competition for the better water, and Jack used me to hold pools for his clients. When I questioned the ethics of it, he said, "Zane Grey did it," and that settled that. I was supposed to stand at the head of the pool and fiddle with my tackle or cast a fly-less floating line, but under no circumstances was I to disturb the fish. Well, that was asking a lot, and the fact was, I had splendid fishing, though I would have enjoyed it more if I could have shared it with Jack—the beauty of those silver fish swirling onto the fly, leaping into the air—because it was a great joy to see his face light up in the way that a fish story, and *only* a fish story, could ignite it. I felt only slightly guilty. Yes, I cheated on him, but he'd insulted me and my fishing needs by suggesting that I, a serious fly-fisherman, should or even *could* stand beside a beautiful pool, fly-rod in hand, and not use it. Who did he think I was? I certainly didn't drive all that distance every weekend for the sex.

In mid-summer, when the fishing slowed, I quit visiting so often. Business at the shop was picking up, and Patrick was weary of weekend duty. Also, he found it stressful having his work critiqued in his presence by patrons, who, in his opinion, didn't know diddly about art *or* fish. He had a tendency to try to educate his critics, and it wasn't good for sales. He needed a break, and more time to paint, sculpt, and fish. "Of course, you need a break," I said, generous now that I had caught my fish. "Take all the time you want."

Perhaps if we'd charged an admission fee, we might have shown a profit. Many people came on their lunch breaks to look, touch, test rods, or talk fishing. Or maybe we should have served food in addition to the coffee. I wanted people to be comfortable. I was working to create an ambience; sell the ambience and the fishing tackle would take care of itself. I believe it would have too, if Jack hadn't returned that fall so full of fire and brimstone. To some extent I blame myself; I left the man alone too long on his river. It affected his mind.

He let his hair and beard grow, and he had a crazy glint in his eye. He looked like Moses and talked like Martin Luther King. He'd had a dream: maybe it wasn't possible to remove the dam through politics as usual, and dynamite, he'd finally realized, was impractical. Therefore, why not have the Augusta dam declared a public nuisance by referendum. "Free the Kennebec 150" was his slogan appended to his petition, 150 being the approximate mileage from Moosehead Lake to Merrymeeting Bay.

I tried to be supportive. I said, "Ok, we'll leave a petition by the cash register, and another by the coffee pot. That way they can't be missed." Jack was skeptical, but pressure for a sale or a signature was antithetical to all that I'd been working for.

"All right," he said. "We'll try it your way first."

The first week we got three signatures—mine, Patrick's and one customer's. "Do you know how many signatures it takes to bring an issue to referendum?" Jack asked.

"More than three?"

"I'm glad you think it's funny."

"Do you have to take everything so seriously? Try and relax. You've been away."

But he couldn't relax, and he couldn't remain in his work area, never mind my suggestions that, until he readjusted to being around people, and until he trimmed his hair and beard, in his work area was exactly where he ought to remain. For my part, I promised to be more aggressive with his petitions. And I was. "Here's another item you might be interested in," I would say, always *after* the sale.

This did not satisfy Jack. So he cut his hair and beard—did it himself, so clumsily that he looked even more like a lunatic—and started mingling with the customers, always with petition in hand, and the same deranged look in his eyes. If a customer made a purchase, Jack would wait until after the sale to make his pitch, but a customer who didn't make a purchase was likely to be followed out of the store and down the sidewalk by Jack brandishing his petition. One time he accused a man of "moral cowardice."

"Jack," I said, as calmly as possible, "that man was on the verge of buying an expensive rod. I've been working with him for weeks."

"Anybody that wishy-washy, we don't need their business."

"We need everybody's business."

"That's all you care about, isn't it? Goddamn bottom line, the almighty dollar. You don't really care about the river, do you?"

"You guide for free now?"

"You're just like the rest of them. You're like the power company."

"You're right, Jack. You're absolutely right. No one cares about that river except you. You're the river's only friend. I hope you two will be very happy together. Would you mind watching the shop for a few minutes? Thank you."

I grabbed my favorite eight-weight Sage and marched across the catwalk to the casting platform. The river is tidal and quite wide in Hallowell. The far shore was a blur of grays and browns. The water was high, slow, and dotted with clumps of foam from the mills. I used the clumps as casting targets, cried and asked myself, "Why can't we protect our men from themselves? Why must they resist? I *demand* an answer."

That winter the living room wasn't nearly large enough; so I enlarged it. I knocked out the wall to the kitchen. Still not large enough. I knocked out another wall. "One more wall, you'll be outside," Jack said.

"That's a thought," I said, sledgehammer in hand.

But Jack's and my life together did not end in violence of that sort. It ended with an act of God. It ended with the Flood of '87, the Hundred Year Flood of the Kennebec. They marked the high water with a plaque on the back of our shop. I thought they should have put our names on it, along with the dates of our life together.

> Jack Michaud
> Anna Cameron
> 6/3/85–4/1/87

Otherwise how would anyone know?

Let the record show that *I* ended it. He never would have said, "Leave," but he would have kept tugging at me, taking line, while I kept trying to bring him closer. We would have fought to the point of exhaustion. The only ethical thing to do in that situation is to break it off, to let him go.

The night before the river crested, we sat up late watching TV footage of the rising water. Jack edged closer and closer to the set until he was sitting a few feet away. This natural disaster, this catastrophe that carried off trees, houses and one casting platform, moved Jack to tears, but joyous tears! His beloved river was taking revenge on all those who had tried to throttle it, or, I suppose, throttle him. Huge brown waves the size of wall-tents moved like an encampment out to sea.

The Augusta dam was under several feet of water. When the water receded the dam would still be standing, but for the moment it was damming nothing. Jack cheered and clenched his fists. His dream was finally realized, if only for a few hours, which, if you think about it, is probably above average.

Then the sports came on. Against everybody's better judgement, the Red Sox were about to start another season. Jack turned the TV off and sat for a while on the floor. I was on the sofa behind him. The room was dark except for the small light over the kitchen sink, now the living room sink. "Anna," Jack said, after we had sat a while, "I'm sorry that I'm not cut out to be a businessman."

"And I'm sorry if I tried to turn you into one," I said.

"I know you wanted the best for me, but I'm just a fishing guide. And fly-tier and rod-builder. I'll never be more than that. Or less."

"Oh, I don't know. You'd make a hell of a preacher."

"Ha, and I'm no politician either. I finally figured that out." He turned and looked at me. "The best thing I can do, probably the only thing I can do for that river is take people fishing on it. Let them see for themselves what it's like and decide if it's worth saving. If they can't see it for themselves, nothing I say is going to make a difference. In the end, people will get the river they deserve."

I didn't say anything to that. It sounded like something he might have read in a magazine. Or maybe it was the beginning of wisdom. Either way, it sounded like good-by.

"You want me to help clean out the shop in the morning?" I asked. It was getting harder to talk.

"Patrick and I can manage. Thank you, though."

"You're welcome. I think I'll toodle off to bed now, if you don't mind."

"Anna…"

Jack was up at first light, whistling as he left the house. "What's he so happy about?" I asked myself. "It's not *all* insured."

I got up, fixed a cup of coffee, ripped a page off the calendar and realized why he was whistling. It was April first, April Fool's Day, but, more to the point, it was the first day of open-water fishing season. My father always went on opening day, never mind that in Maine most waters were still frozen. He'd find a little open place, or failing that, make one. Then he'd wet his line, his feet, freeze his hands, and return home shivering and jubilant, ready now to drill a few teeth for the home team. It's a disease, this fishing, but it's not the afflicted who suffer. It's the next of kin.

So I may have been the only person in the state of Maine neither surprised nor particularly amused when, later that morning, the TV cameras caught Jack and Patrick paddling out of their flooded shop in float-tubes and waders, their rods strung and ready. They took opposite sides of the street and started working slowly downstream, casting to "structure," in this case store fronts and submerged cars.

"Any luck?" the reporter asked when Jack passed their boat.

"Just started," Jack said without taking his eyes off his fly.

"What're you fishing for, antiques?" There was a reaction shot of the reporter laughing at his own joke, the joke being that Hallowell was the antique district.

"Brown trout," Jack said seriously.

"You're kidding."

"Nope, there are a lot of browns in the Kennebec. Hard to find 'em in this high water, but they're in here."

I had to laugh. To Jack, the Flood of the Century was "high water," memorable because it made fish difficult to find.

Jack continued with the reporter. "People don't realize what a great river this is, or could be if it was treated right. They think it's part of the sewer system. They forget it carries fish, and it could carry a whole lot more if it was taken care of. It could be the best fishing anywhere."

There was another reaction shot of the newsman, this time bemused, not quite sure what to think.

"Look down there," Jack said. "See how that water swirls around the corner of that building. See that slick water in the center? That's good holding water for trout." He began laying out more line, one lovely false cast after another—tight loop, no wasted motion, beautiful to watch.

The fly landed in the center of the slick. The camera man panned to the reporter, who now had a strange expectant look on his face. Either he was a much better actor than I thought, or Jack had him believing that a large brown trout was about to rise at the corner of Water Street and Elm.

Thomaston U.

I don't know what it's like for other first-time offenders, but the night before my first crime, I couldn't sleep. So while Janine was still snoring away, I left the house to make my rounds and say my goodbyes.

I parked on the bridge below the paper mill, got out and looked upriver. Like most people, I bitched and moaned about the mill, the stink and noise, but now, gazing upon it for what was likely my last time in years, I realized the mill radiated a sort of industrial charm. It's mercury vapor lamps cast an eerie glow, as if the mill were basking in its own moonlight. There was a certain majesty to the enormous mounds of pulp and wood chips, and the warning lights atop the tallest smokestack twinkled like stars in a misty sky. Granted that it wasn't a scene likely to find its way onto calendars depicting the beauty of rural Maine, I still found it moving and felt a lump form in my throat.

Then a Rumford police car pulled up beside me. "Oh shit," I thought. "They read my mind." I was on my way to rob a bank, see. I even had my weapon on my person. It wasn't real—a water pistol painted black and weighted with sand—but just the same...

Then the officer rolled down the window, and I breathed a sigh of relief. It was Cecil Ouellette, a simple soul I'd known all my life. I said, "Good morning, Cecil. What's up?"

He shined the flashlight into my face, a totally unnecessary move, since the mill illuminated the entire terrain. "Dibble?" he asked. "Leonard Dibble, is that you?"

"Of course, it's me. It's my car, isn't it?" My blue Chevy Citation was locally famous. It was a Citation in name only, all its innards having been replaced, enlarged, or improved. It was bursting at the seams with power. It reminded me of a crab that had outgrown its shell and was about to shed.

"What happened to your hair, your beard?"

"Oh," I said, "I got tired of long hair. Thought I'd try a different style. Maybe change my luck with the ladies." It was a gesture of disguise. Also, I'd heard unpleasant stories about prison barbers.

Cecil hoisted himself out of the car, came over and stood beside me. "Are you all right?" he asked.

"Course I am. Just couldn't sleep, that's all. Had some things on my mind."

"I guess this economy has sort of got everybody down," he said.

"Not me," I said. "A recession is good for auto repair. People fix up instead of buy new."

"Hadn't thought of that."

I didn't say it, but I was sick of fixing cars. I wanted to better myself, but didn't know how. I needed time to read and re-educate myself. Four years was about what I had in mind.

Cecil put a comforting hand on my shoulder. "Things OK at home?"

I shrugged. "About average." Janine and I hadn't slept in the same room for weeks, but it was none of Cecil's business where I slept.

"Janine all right?"

"Yep, she's fine. Well, she has put on a couple of more pounds."

He shook his head. "What's wrong with that woman?"

"I don't know, likes to eat, I guess." Actually I did know, but I was sworn to secrecy. She was trying to eat her way onto disability. It's hard for working people to understand, but the U.S. Government will actually pay you for being fat and having high blood pressure. I didn't approve of her plan, but I had to admit that if it hadn't been for Janine's way of seeing things, I would never have come up with the idea of prison as an entitlement program.

Cecil was struggling for words, looking around, scraping his shoes on the railing. "I have to ask you this, Leonard."

"What's that?"

He turned and look straight at me. "You weren't thinking of jumping, were you?"

"Are you kidding?" I asked, looking down at the filthy Androscoggin. "A man could drown in that river. And if he didn't drown, the pollution would kill him."

He chuckled. "Well, it's a lot cleaner than it used to be. State's talking of putting trout in there again."

"Really?" First I'd heard of that. I liked trout, and they figured into my future. It looked like all the pieces were falling into place.

"I had to ask, you know? I'd be remiss if I didn't ask."

"I understand. You're just doing your job." Then I looked back towards the mill. "You know, Cecil, I've lived here all my life, and I don't think I've ever really looked at that mill before. It's kind of pretty in a way, don't you agree?"

He looked at the mill, then back at me. "Are you *sure* you're all right?"

"I'm fine, Cecil. Best I've felt in some time."

He looked back at the mill and shook his head. "Only thing pretty about that place is the payroll, and sometimes I'm not sure it's worth it." Cecil climbed back into his cruiser and cranked the engine. It purred like a cat. It ought to have; I tuned it myself. "Don't let me catch you up here when the shift changes," he said. "Some of those boys are so bleary-eyed they might knock you off that bridge and not even notice. Or care."

"I'm on my way," I said.

So as not to raise further suspicions, I drove down to West Peru to Barney's Auto Repair, of which I was sole proprietor, Barney having been dead for a number of years. But what kind of name was Leonard for an auto shop? For anything? Besides, I never had the same attachment to the place that Barney had. My attachment was to Barney. His was to my mother, and through her, to me, which was how I got into auto repair in the first place. It wasn't until Barney was dead for a few years that I realized how little I liked working on cars other than my own. That was different. That wasn't work; it was personal grooming.

I spent the next few hours washing and waxing, changing the oil, freshening the anti-freeze, checking air pressure in the tires, and polishing the interior. Before I pulled out of the garage and onto the highway, I sat for a long time with the engine running, revving it, letting it idle, revving it, letting it idle. The engine beat like a heart against the bottom of my foot.

There're more banks in our town than there are churches. Janine said that was exactly as it ought to be, banks being a better index of our true religion. Certainly in her case that was correct.

Androscoggin Savings & Loan was a squat brick building with a single drive-up window and small lobby. Inside, a cluster of customers waited for the next available teller. At first I couldn't decide whether to cut in or wait my turn. Criminality came more naturally to me than rudeness. Then I noticed this logger a few places ahead of me in line. He was a rugged, stocky man in worn jeans, flannel shirt and steel-toed boots. I'd seen a pulp truck outside. He'd probably just dropped a load of wood off at the mill and was here to deposit the proceeds. I was about to cut in front when I noticed the knuckles on both his hands were bleeding. The skin was knocked completely off one place, and he didn't even seem to notice. I didn't like the looks of that. A man that insensitive to pain could be a threat. If those had been my hands, there would've been BandAids everywhere. I hated banged knuckles. Some years it seemed like carmakers competed to see who could do the best job of hiding spark plugs. So I decided to wait until that fellow finished his business.

When his time finally came, he took forever signing his name, and it wasn't because of the condition of his knuckles. The man could probably carry a hundred-pound stick of wood like a loaf of bread, but he could barely write his own name. His jaw clenched from the effort. He formed each letter with childlike precision.

I felt so sorry for him that I wanted to take him by the shoulders and shake him and say, "You best leave that logging truck behind and follow me. There's a better life ahead, for both of us!" But I doubt he would've listened. Some people wouldn't see prison as a way of improving themselves, because they don't know where in life to look for possibility. Janine taught me that. And maybe it wasn't fair, but this fellow struck me as someone whose idea of heaven was a paid-off pulp truck swaying beneath a full load of spruce.

When my turn came, I handed the teller a typed note, which said, "Do not let on that you are being robbed. Just clean out the cash drawer and dump the money into my shopping bag." Then I spied three moneybags outside a time-locked vault. "And I'll have one of those, too," I added. I opened my jacket just wide enough for her to see the pistol butt protruding from my belt.

The teller, Lynda, was a real pro for such a young lady. When she saw the gun, she stiffened slightly, cocked her head to one side, took a deep breath and pushed away from the counter like an athlete entering the big game in a crucial situation. And why not? She'd been trained for this moment. (And I knew what that training was: observe and cooperate; do not resist) Now she had a chance to apply that training, to demonstrate what a poised professional she really was. She might even parlay her performance into a promotion.

Lynda calmly and efficiently collected the money, careful not to alert the other employees or the customers. Then she deposited the money into my bag and shoved it across to me. "Will that be all today?" she asked in a voice identical to that which she had used with previous customers.

"I think that will be it for today," I said. Then I winked, because at that point I felt that she and I were in this together, that we had the male and female leads in the most important production of our lives. It's possible that I misread the situation, because she did not wink back.

I slid a second note across to her. It said, "One person posing as a customer is actually my accomplice. If you behave and don't hit the alarm for ten minutes after I leave, you will never know which one it is." Then I turned and walked calmly out of the bank and around the corner to my waiting car.

I saw this movie once, in which a man has just been released from prison. He is standing all alone outside the thick, high prison walls. That's all we see behind him, enormous slabs of stone and brick, steel doors. Before him lie empty streets slick with rain. No one is waiting for him. In one hand he holds a little satchel, which we presume contains all his earthly possessions. He pulls the collar of his raincoat up around his neck, and the camera closes in on his face. He squints his eyes, and, just when we think that maybe he is going to cry, the tiniest trace of a smile sneaks across his face. And that was exactly how I felt as I stepped out of that bank onto the streets of my new life.

See, I believe that a man is entitled to try and improve his station in life, is obligated to, so long as he doesn't bring undue harm to his fellow man, and who got hurt by the little bit of money I stole? It was all insured by the U.S. Government, the same U.S. Government that pays people for being fat. So don't talk to me about crime. Call your congressman.

People underestimate me, always have. They see the dirt and grease on my hands, the grimy overalls, they give me looks. Soon they would be saying things like, "He robbed a bank in broad daylight not twenty minutes from his home, gave all the money away, and got caught in twenty-four hours! How much brains could he have?"

More than they thought. I knew that when I left the money outside of All Souls Shelter that not everyone who took some would return it, when they learned that it was stolen. (And I certainly didn't need to worry about Janine returning the little bit that I left her) If the authorities couldn't determine how much I gave away, they couldn't tell how much I kept, now, could they?

I kept eight thousand dollars, nothing larger than a fifty. I stuffed it into a Tupperware container. Janine swore by Tupperware; she said things would keep forever, and when it came to food storage or consumption, she was the authority. Then I drove up to Coos Canyon, along the relatively pristine Swift River, a tributary of the Androscoggin, and a favorite place of mine. Janine and I used to come here before we were married, and, for a while, after we were married. I would fish, and she would pan for gold, and fuss at me

"What are you wasting your time fishing for, when you could be helping me?" she'd ask. "With your help, we could find twice as much."

"You don't know everything I'm doing. You can't see inside my head." Fly-fishing was when I had some of my best thoughts.

"See into it? Heck, I can see through it."

Like I say, people underestimate me.

The soil is too thin for burying things up here, and every spring the frost heaves up whatever is closest to the surface. So I tucked the Tupperware into the crotch of an old-growth pine above eye-level. I covered the carton with pine needles and debris, tucked it in and told it good night. I would see it in a few years.

I brought my fly-rod along. I hadn't used it for years, but I would miss at least the possibility of going fishing. Also that fly-rod figured into my future. My hand fit perfectly into the worn cork handle; it showed me how to hold it. I clambered down the steep rock wall to the water and made a few ceremonial casts with the same ragged fly that had been tied on for years. The hook was rusted and the fly so battered that I couldn't recognize the pattern.

It didn't matter. There weren't any fish left in the river anyway, and never had been many, and most of those were tiny. But they were native brook trout and every bit as beautiful to me as the tiny flecks of gold that Janine made such a fuss over. She kept her head so mired in her gold-panning that she missed the whole point of the river—the beauty of clear water flowing over different colored stones, the jewel-like little trout. I tried to explain, "A river shouldn't have to make you wealthy to enrich your spirit." I actually used to talk like that before she broke me of the habit. Well, she didn't break me of the habit; my life did. I just blamed her.

When Barney died, my work load more than doubled. I wanted to take on another man, but Janine, who did the books, said that we couldn't afford it. "Barney could," I said.

"Not until he was old," she said, and she had the numbers to prove it. There was enough income to support one family whose possessions were already paid for and one on the way up, but not enough to support two just starting out in life. And we had things we wanted. I mean, *already* had them—a house, two cars, a pair of snowmobiles, and a satellite dish. We just hadn't gotten around to paying for them yet, and we never would if we had to hire another man.

One day I gently suggested to Janine that maybe she could get an outside job. "Part time, you know. Doing hair." She was good at that.

"Who would do your books?" she asked, clearly hurt. "You'd have to hire somebody. They'd probably steal you blind. In the long run it would cost you more than you would save."

"Then you think of something!" I said. I was sick of being buried in work I didn't love.

And that was when Janine came up with the bright idea of getting disability. She had snitched a handbook from her doctor's office that told exactly what you had to do to qualify. When she discovered the section on obesity, she shrieked the same way she did when she found gold. She'd always had high blood pressure, and she loved to eat. "I'm halfway there already!" she shouted.

To celebrate, she had two huge slices of lemon meringue pie and a liter of Pepsi. I had a beer. Then a few more. I realized, you cannot ask someone else, even your wife, especially your wife, to rescue you from your own life.

Towards evening, fishless, I reeled in and climbed slowly, hand over hand, out of the canyon. At sundown I unfurled my sleeping-bag on a bed of pine needles, and built a small fire. It was early September, the air was cool and, upwind of the mill, smelled of pine and damp soil. Best of all, there were no biting insects. In the background was the steady trickle of the river as it percolated through the canyon. Flowing water always had a powerful, soothing effect on me, and I slept soundly until sunup, when Cecil Ouellette's cruiser pulled in and parked beside my truck. No sirens or flashing lights—that was Cecil. In a day when every volunteer fireman and paramedic decorated their vehicles with racks of lights and accessories, Cecil scrupulously avoided theatrics. The man had standards, and I admired him for it.

He moseyed over to where I was trying to re-kindle a small fire, and said, "Figured I'd find you here. You always did like this place."

"Little out of your jurisdiction, isn't it?"

"Well, the state boys are too busy interviewing witnesses, collecting evidence, doing forensics—they're even putting together a composite sketch." He chuckled at the bureaucratic silliness.

"You want some coffee? I'll have this water hot in no time." Nothing burns like dried pine twigs or smells so sweet.

"I have a cup in the car."

"Just one?"

He nodded. "Sorry." Then added. "I sort of blame myself. I knew something was wrong yesterday when I saw you on that bridge. I said, 'Cecil, that's not normal behavior. You've known that man all your life, and that is not something he'd be doing.' I should've stopped you."

Until you meet an officer like Cecil Ouellette, it is easy to forget that police are here to help, same as doctors and nurses. "Don't blame yourself," I said. "Besides, what makes you think I had anything to do with that bank? Assuming that's what you're talking about."

"*Three* different people in that bank recognized you. *Two* were former customers. You *worked* on their cars!"

I thought for a moment, but drew a blank. "Describe their vehicles, and maybe it'll come back to me."

Cecil skipped the formalities, except for my Miranda rights. He read me those, but his heart wasn't in it. He didn't bother with handcuffs, and he even allowed me to ride in the front seat. We stopped for more coffee, and at the station, he didn't tell me that I was entitled to one phone call. He said, "Call Janine. The woman is worried sick."

"Ok, but first you have to promise you'll stop blaming yourself, awright? I knew what I was doing." This part I had not figured on. Using a fake gun, I knew that if anything went wrong, the only person shot would be me. I hadn't thought of Cecil's feelings as collateral damage. "None of this is your fault."

I called Janine and told her that in the glove box of her car she would find five hundred dollars. She was to keep a hundred for herself and use the rest to buy books. "Fly-fishing books, fly-tying books, and catalogues—I need fly-tying materials." Fly-fishing was the last pure thing I could remember; it seemed like the place to start.

"I could be arrested for receiving stolen property," Janine said.

"That money could just as easily have come from the shop."

"Say it did, Lenny. Tell me that it did."

"I go by 'Leon' now," I said, "and that money most definitely came from the shop." After bank-robbery, lying came surprisingly easy.

"'Leon,'" she said, testing the sound of it. "'Leon.' I like that. Why didn't you go by Leon before?"

"I don't know. I just never thought of it before."

I had a private cell. It was built semi-private, but the census was low. After deer season, when winter closed in, you wouldn't get a private cell any where in Maine. I'd been told that all the cells at Thomaston were semi-private except the ones you didn't want any part of. I'd also heard that Thomaston had one of the finest prison libraries in the East—row after row of books, stacked to the ceiling—and that prisoners had unlimited time to read. It was like a huge university without professors, and the entrance requirements were so incredibly lax! I had to laugh. Janine spent so much time scheming and conniving, and all I had to do to get my way was rob one bank.

I had a vision of my incarcerated self—though in the vision, the self felt surprisingly free. I could see me reading books and tying flies, and teaching others to tie, and to cast and to fish. To me nothing seemed less compatible with crime than fly-fishing. I'd offer a secular alternative to the usual religious stuff they fed prisoners. Only later would my converts realize that fly-fishing was not so secular after all, but was as good a route to God as any.

The day would come when the locals would say of me, "He was doing OK until he took a wrong turn in life," and they'd be right, but the "wrong turn" wasn't robbing the bank. It was abandoning the river, the water and the trout in favor of so-called "earthly rewards."

A few days later Janine came by with a duffel bag full of books. Well, almost full. "That doesn't look like four hundred dollars worth of books to me."

"It's hard to find four hundred dollars worth of fly-fishing books around here," she said. "Besides, the guards rummaged all through it. Who knows what they removed?"

I smiled. Same old Janine.

We were sitting on opposite sides of a plexiglass partition talking into speakers. She was wearing a cotton, print dress the size of a small tent. She'd fixed her hair and put on make-up, even a little eye shadow. She had nice brown eyes; she looked good. There was just too much of her. Her features looked like they'd been painted onto the side of a balloon. Deflated, she would have been pretty again.

"You're all over the news," she said. "You're the talk of the town."

"I bet."

"Can't say it's been entirely complimentary, though."

"Well, you know how people are around here, Janine. You rob one little bank, and they start dragging your name through the mud."

"She smiled. "Some of it's been favorable. They say, 'He *seemed* like such a nice person…do anything in the world for you…come out in the freezing cold and start your car…'"

"No more of that, thank God." That had been the first responsibility Barney had given me, "dawn patrol." At the time it seemed like an honor.

Janine leaned forward and whispered into the speaker. "I don't know exactly why you did what you did, Lenny, Leon, but I know you must have had good reason, because it *seems* to agree with you. I could hear it on the phone. Your voice sounded sure and strong. And I see it in your eyes now. They look clear and more determined. You remind me of someone. You know who I mean?"

I nodded. She meant that I reminded her of me, years ago. It looked like I had accidentally regained the respect from her that I didn't even know I'd lost. How peculiar. Janine craved money. I hungered for time, but I was the one who robbed the bank. Of course, I didn't do it for the money. I did it for the fringe benefits, but she didn't know that.

"You don't have to say anything," she said. "I just want you to know that I'm proud of you. And a little bit ashamed of myself."

"No need for that."

"How much time do you think you'll get?"

"Well, if my research is correct, I'll be sentenced to eight to ten, but probably only serve a small portion." I planned to be an exemplary prisoner.

"However long it is," Janine said, "when you get out, I'll be waiting for you. And I'll be thin too. Well, maybe not thin, but, you know, like I was."

"You don't have to do that."

"Well, I'm going to."

I didn't say any more. Who knew how much time I'd get, or where'd I'd go, or whether she would be there or not, or how much she would weigh? But I liked hearing her say it.

It was funny, but sitting there separated from Janine by that thick slab of plexiglass, I felt closer to her than I had in a long time. It was like this barrier had between us all along, and now that it was visible, we could look through it to each other. And now that I had lain aside one of my false selves, I could see it was more than her weight that had come between us. And she could see it too, and it made her eyes shine with hope, and, I guess, love. We pressed our hands against the plexiglass, fitting each finger to the other, like people did in movies—we didn't know how else to act—and it didn't matter that her fingers were puffy as little sausages or that mine were still tatooed with grime. Then the guard said it was time for her to go, and we each cried a little, but not so anyone else would notice.

That night for the first time throughout the whole ordeal, I felt afraid. I felt overwhelmed by my own ignorance, which seemed more enormous than ever. Imagine—love lurking in my own fat wife! What lay ahead? I was half afraid to look, and yet I couldn't' take my eyes off the future. I felt woozy and disoriented. The air seemed thin like mountain air, without enough oxygen. I lay on my bunk, clutching the bag of books to my chest like a large stuffed animal and tried to sleep. Towards morning a late summer thunderstorm rolled through. It shook the windows and made the jail tremble. It felt like the whole building was in motion, like a train passing over a rough rail bed, like a locomotive pulling ever so slowly away from the station.

978-0-595-37288-1
0-595-37288-0